Mary-Kate
and Ashley

mary-kate olsen   ashley olsen

so little time

Check out these other great
so little time
titles:

mary-kate olsen   **ashley** olsen

so little time

best friends forever

By Nancy Butcher

Based on the series Created by Eric Cohen
and Tonya Hurley

Based on the teleplay Written by Patrick McCarthy
& Erik Shapiro

▄▄ HarperEntertainment
An Imprint of HarperCollinsPublishers

A PARACHUTE PRESS BOOK

A PARACHUTE PRESS BOOK

Parachute Publishing, L.L.C.
156 Fifth Avenue, Suite 302
New York, NY 10010

Published by
■HarperEntertainment
An *Imprint* of HarperCollins*Publishers*
10 East 53rd Street, New York, NY 10022-5299

ISBN 0-06-009316-1

HarperCollins®, ■®, and HarperEntertainment™ are trademarks of HarperCollins Publishers Inc.

First printing: November 2003

Printed in the United States of America

Visit HarperEntertainment on the World Wide Web at
www.harpercollins.com

10 9 8 7 6 5 4 3 2 1 .

chapter
one

"A, A, A," fourteen-year-old Riley Carlson chanted quietly to herself. She hoped the grade gods were listening to her.

Her twin sister, Chloe, turned around in her seat. "What are you mumbling back there?" she whispered.

"I'm wishing for an A on this paper," Riley whispered back. "I need it to bring my grade up from a C to a B."

Chloe flipped her wavy blond hair over her shoulders. "Something tells me it's a little too late for that," she said. "Miss Westmore is already handing back our papers."

It was third period at West Malibu High School, and the sisters were in business studies class. Their teacher was walking up and down the aisles, passing back the students' papers from last week. The topic had been "Successful Marketing and Advertising." In Riley's humble opinion a topic like "How to Make a Million Dollars

Overnight" would have been way more interesting and practical, but she was the student, not the teacher. Oh, well.

Riley watched nervously as Miss Westmore started down her aisle. She tried to read the teacher's facial expression and body language. It was a sure way to tell who was getting what grade.

Miss Westmore grinned as she handed Blaine Snyder her paper. Blaine the Brain probably got an A, Riley thought.

"Very good comparison of different perfume ads, Blaine," Miss Westmore said.

Connor Roohan was next. Miss Westmore smiled so broadly that you could see all her teeth and practically her tonsils, too. Definitely an A-plus, Riley thought.

"Excellent analysis of Internet marketing strategies, Connor," Miss Westmore praised him.

Then it was Chloe's turn. Miss Westmore gave Chloe a closed-mouth smile. Probably an A-minus or maybe a B-plus.

"I would have liked a little more on *why* recording companies should hand out free CD samples at high schools," Miss Westmore told her.

"Isn't it, like, obvious?" a girl from across the room called out.

Riley was next. Miss Westmore glanced down at her pile of papers and pressed her lips together in a tight, thin line.

Riley squirmed in her seat. This didn't look good. Come on, Miss Westmore, smile! *Smile*!

"This would have been a much stronger paper if you'd done more than simply describe all the television infomercials you watched over a twelve-hour period," Miss Westmore said.

Riley shook her head. "No, no, that wasn't the point! I was trying to explore the, um, universal theme of, um…"

But Miss Westmore had already handed Riley her paper and moved on to the girl sitting behind her.

Riley took a deep breath and made herself look at the grade.

It was a B-minus.

[<u>Riley</u>: Right about now you're probably thinking: The girl watches TV for twelve straight hours and writes about it, and she expects an A? Okay, so maybe I could have come up with something better, like why Symphony jeans ads make me want to throw up. Still, Miss Westmore should have given me points for my brilliant compare-and-contrast of morning versus late-night infomercials.]

Chloe turned around in her seat. "Bad news?" she asked.

Riley nodded. "Bad. Awful. The pits."

Chloe gave her a sympathetic look.

Riley glanced around the room to see how their friends were doing. Larry Slotnick was pumping a fist in the air. Definitely an A. Sierra Pomeroy and Tara Jordan were both grinning. B-pluses, at least.

"Now for your next assignment…" Miss Westmore said to the class when she'd finished handing out the papers.

A chorus of groans rose in the air.

Riley sat up a little straighter. Maybe this new assignment would give her a chance to save her dying grade. She twirled a strand of blond hair around her finger and waited eagerly.

"For this assignment you're going to split into teams of your choosing," Miss Westmore began. "Six people, maximum. Each team will start a small business together. You'll create a product—any product—and market it, using the strategies we've been studying. Then, a week from Monday, each team will set up booths in the main hallway by the auditorium and sell its product. Whichever team makes the biggest profit wins."

Larry raised his hand. "What's the grand prize?" he asked. "A Porsche convertible? A trip to Baja?"

"An A-plus," Miss Westmore replied.

Yes! Riley thought. This is excellent. I am *so* going to get that A-plus. But first I have to pick my own personal dream team.

"Okay, class," Miss Westmore called out. "I'm going to leave it to you to choose your teams. Once you've got your group together, I want you to spend the remaining class time brainstorming ideas for your product."

Chloe turned around, her blue eyes sparkling. "Hey! Why don't we be a team?" she suggested to Riley.

[Riley: Now, normally I would say yes in two seconds. Chloe is family! But today I have to think about it. I mean, is my sister dream team material...? Duh! She got a better grade than I did. Okay, so it took me three seconds this time!]

"Sure!" Riley said to Chloe.

"Hey, can we join you guys?"

Riley looked up. Sierra and Tara were standing by her desk.

Sierra Pomeroy was Riley's best friend. She was wearing white cargo pants and a black rhinestone-studded T-shirt that showed off her flaming red hair.

At home, Sierra went by her real name, Sarah, and wore conservative clothes to please her parents. But each morning at school, "Sarah" slipped into the girls' bathroom, changed into some really hip outfit she had smuggled in her backpack, and instantly became Sierra.

Tara Jordan was closer to Chloe than Riley, although they all hung out together. Tara had a great sense of humor. Today she was wearing jeans and a powder blue top with a big red heart on it.

"Definitely!" Chloe said before Riley had a chance to reply. "The four of us will make an awesome team. Hey, Tara, did you get that E-mail I sent you this morning?"

Tara nodded. "I can't *believe* Kevin had the nerve to

break up with Jessica over the phone!" she exclaimed. "What a jerk."

"Are you guys talking about Kevin Young and Jessica Robinson?" Sierra piped up.

Time out! Riley wanted to say. She wasn't getting a chance to pick her team; her team was picking *her*. Sure, Chloe was her sister and Sierra was her best friend and Tara was a close friend, too. But would they help her score that all-important A-plus? Maybe she would be better off with Blaine the Brain or Connor Roohan, speaking strictly from an academic standpoint. When it came to grades, it was every girl for herself.

"Hey, guys, can I join your team?" Larry pulled up a chair next to Riley and gazed into her eyes. Larry was the Carlsons' goofy next-door neighbor. He'd had a crush on Riley since first grade, but Riley liked him only as a friend.

Larry? On her team? Riley took a deep breath. She would have to give this one a lot of thought. Maybe get back to him tomorrow…

"Hey, Larry. What did you get on your paper?" Tara asked him.

Larry grinned. "Just call me Larry A-*plus* Slotnick."

Riley did a mental double take. "Sure, Larry, we'd love to have you on our team!" she said quickly.

Now that that was settled, it was time to get down to business. Riley reached into her backpack and whipped out a notebook and a pen. Larry, Sierra, Tara, and Chloe did the same.

"Okay," Riley said, poising her pen over a fresh page in her book. "First we have to come up with a killer product for our business. Does anyone have any ideas?"

"You can't go wrong with makeup," Sierra said, studying her nails. "Maybe we can invent a new kind of nail polish. Hey, Riles, remember that time we stayed up all night giving each other pedicures with weird-name colors like Oil Slick and Algae?"

Riley giggled. That was one of their best sleepovers ever.

"How about *recycled* nail polish?" Chloe piped up.

"Nail polish made from garbage!" Larry cried out.

Riley had to admit that, despite her initial reservations, this felt right. Maybe we'll be an awesome team after all. Working together with your buds *had* to be better than working with kids you hardly knew.

"Speaking of garbage, has anyone heard the new Junkyard single?" Tara spoke up.

"'Don't Throw Me Away.' It's so cool," Chloe said.

Okay, the discussion was losing focus. Riley tapped her pen against her desk. "People, we need to stick to the topic," she said. "Let's brainstorm more ideas. How about clothes? Or school supplies?"

"Oh! Speaking of bands, you all know who's going to be in Malibu in two weeks, right?" Chloe exclaimed. "Only Crash, my favorite group in the world. Except the tickets will probably be impossible to get." She sighed.

"Chloe, listen!" Tara said. "My dad said he might be

able to snag me two tickets. If he can, do you want to go with me?"

"*Do* I *want to go with you*?" Chloe practically screeched.

Miss Westmore gave her an icy look from across the room.

"Do I want to go with you?" Chloe whispered. "Is the earth round? Do I like pineapple pizza? Am I a natural blond? The answer is *yes*!"

Tara's father worked in the music industry and could often get rare tickets to superhot concerts. Riley was happy for Chloe, but she wanted to get back to the assignment.

"That is so great, Chloe," Riley said. "So what would you think of creating a food product? Rainbow-colored brownies? New and improved lunch meat?"

But no one on her team was listening. They were too busy talking about the Crash concert.

Okay, if this keeps up, my grade in this class is going to be...*lunch meat*, Riley thought with a sinking heart.

"I'm going to the Crash concert, I'm going to the Crash concert," Chloe sang after school. She was so totally psyched, she couldn't help rubbing it in just a little.

But Riley didn't react. In fact, she didn't say anything as she followed Chloe into their beachfront house.

"Riley? Earth to Riley?" Chloe nudged her. Riley had seemed preoccupied the whole way home from school.

"I'm still trying to come up with the perfect product for our business studies project," Riley told her. "Today is Friday, and we have to set up our booths in, what? Ten days? We don't have a lot of time. And I—I mean, *we*— need to win and get that A-plus!"

"Relax. We'll come up with something," Chloe reassured her. Then she had a brilliant idea. "Hey, I do some of my best thinking when I'm shopping. You want to go to the mall?"

Riley didn't answer her question. "Maybe we should ask Mom for some suggestions," she said. "She knows about this stuff."

[<u>Chloe</u>: **Correction: Our mom doesn't just know about this stuff, she lives and breathes it. You know those crazy-busy business execs who make overseas conference calls at three in the morning? Well, that's our mom. She owns a major fashion design company. You should hear her, switching back and forth between French and Spanish and Mandarin while she's lying in bed in her jams with cucumber cream on her face. We are so proud of her!**]

"So let's ask her," Chloe said. "Mom!" she called.

Chloe dropped her backpack on the floor and glanced around the quiet living room. Something was wrong. The house was *too* quiet. Usually, this time of day, the place was filled with the sounds of her mother gabbing on the phone and frantically composing E-mails on her laptop.

"Mom?" she tried again.

No answer.

Riley frowned. "Mom told me she was meeting a client here at four today. Where is she?"

Just then a terrible, piercing shriek broke the silence.

Chloe and Riley looked at each other.

"Mom!" they both cried.

chapter two

"It came from the kitchen," Chloe said, rushing through the swinging door.

Riley followed her. "Mom, are you okay?" she called out anxiously.

Manuelo was at the stove, but where was their mother? "Manuelo, where's Mom? Why did she scream?" Chloe asked breathlessly.

Manuelo held up a steaming silver teakettle. It had a small silver bird for a spout. "The bird, she was the one who screamed," he explained. "She was letting me know that the water was boiling. So I took her off the stove."

[Chloe: In case you're wondering who Manuelo is, he's part housekeeper, part chef, part live-in therapist. If you're having a bad hair day or a bad boy day, he'll whip up one of his yummy mango smoothies for you, sit you down, and say, "Little one, remember what's really important in life. A family that loves you, good friends, and not putting too much garlic in the pesto."]

"So where's Mom?" Riley asked, looking around.

"Upstairs resting," he said. "I was making some special tea to calm her nerves. It's a recipe that has been in my family for generations."

"Why does Mom need to calm her nerves? She *lives* on nerves," Chloe pointed out.

Manuel sighed. "I have something to tell you, little ones. Your mother got dizzy and almost fainted. I had to call Dr. Schynoll. He left a few minutes ago."

Dr. Schynoll? This did not sound good.

"Is she all right?" Chloe asked, worried.

Manuelo held up a hand. "Your mother is fine, but the doctor said that she's been working too hard. She has too much stress. He ordered her to take a two-week vacation from her job and rest, rest, rest."

"Did she laugh at him?" Riley asked Manuelo.

Manuelo nodded. "Of course! But Dr. Schynoll put his feet down. He told her that if she did not rest, she would only get worse. If her blood pressure continues to rise, she could end up in the hospital!"

The hospital? "I want to see her," Chloe said.

"Your father is with her now. I called him," Manuelo said.

Chloe ran up the stairs, followed by Riley and Manuelo. Macy Carlson was in her room, lying on her bed with a washcloth draped over her forehead. She was dressed in a navy-blue suit and a white silk blouse with a Chinese collar. One stiletto-heeled black shoe was on; the other was on the floor.

Jake Carlson, Chloe and Riley's father, was massaging Macy's bare foot. He was wearing a pair of denim cutoffs and a rumpled gray T-shirt that had had the word BREATHE on it. "Relax," he said to Macy. "This is a new reflexology technique I learned at a wellness retreat in Big Sur."

[**Chloe**: Okay, from this angle it kind of looks like our parents are still together, but they're not. As you can probably tell, Dad's the complete opposite of my mom. Maybe that's why they are separated. They used to run the fashion business together, but Dad needed a simpler life. Now he's living in a nearby trailer park, trying to find himself. He spends a lot of time doing yoga, and he's very, very relaxed. Maybe Mom should take some downtime lessons from him!]

Chloe rushed to her mother's side. Macy's face was pale, and her usually styled-to-the-max brown hair was rumpled. "Mom, we were so worried about you."

"I'm fine," Macy said, struggling to sit up. "Have I gotten any phone calls? I'm expecting a shipment of buttons from Singapore."

Manuelo shook his head. "You must not worry about such things. Here, I brought you a nice tea."

Macy glanced suspiciously at the steaming mug.

She took a tentative sip and frowned. "Can't I have a double espresso instead?"

"No more espressos until you're all better," Jake said firmly. "Caffeine is not what you need right now." He turned to his daughters. "We were just discussing what to do for the next two weeks so your mother can recover properly."

"Can we go to Hawaii?" Riley spoke up. "Mom could get in some serious R and R there."

"How about a spa?" Chloe suggested. "You know, aromatherapy facials, seaweed wraps, hot-stone massages…"

Macy shook her head. "A vacation is out of the question. You girls have school. And I have a business to run." She glanced around anxiously. "Has anyone seen my Palm Pilot?"

"You are *not* running the business for the next two weeks," Jake declared. "I will take over for you until you're back on your feet. And that's final."

"But I'm already feeling better," Macy insisted. "Besides, I have a very important trade show on Saturday. Saturday? Oh, my gosh, that's tomorrow!"

"I'll go in your place," Jake said.

"I'll go with Dad and help out," Riley volunteered.

"And I'll stay here and help you chill out," Chloe offered.

Macy rolled her eyes. "Thank you, family." She smiled at Chloe. "Why don't you find my laptop, honey, and we can get started? I have some E-mails I could dictate to you."

"Mom! I'm going to help you *relax*, not *relapse*," Chloe told her. "As of right this minute, I'm taking everything: your laptop, your cell phone, your Palm Pilot, and all your sketch pads. And no dictating, unless you want to give Manuelo your dinner order. Got it? "

"I will serve only calming foods," Manuelo promised.

Macy looked defeated. "Oh, all right."

Chloe bent down and kissed her mother on the cheek. Then she handed her the remote control to the small TV in the bedroom. "For the next two weeks this is the only electronic device you're allowed to touch!"

Riley took a sip of her hot chocolate with peppermint whipped cream that evening. She, Larry, and Sierra were sitting at a big table in the back of the Newsstand Café.

The Newsstand was one of their favorite hangouts. It always smelled like exotic coffees and cinnamon, and the jukebox was always rocking. Plus it was usually packed with kids from school.

Riley took another, longer sip. She hoped the chocolate would go straight to her brain. Maybe it would help her stop worrying about her mom. Maybe it would also help her come up with a brilliant idea for the big business studies project.

Chloe headed over to their table and plopped into

a chair, holding an armload of magazines. "I'm buying these for Mom. I think they'll help her relax," she said.

"Riley filled us in on your mom's stress meltdown," Sierra said. "Is there anything we can do?"

"I could bring over some of my mom's relaxation tapes," Tara offered. "She listens to them whenever she has to pay bills."

"Thanks, guys. That's really sweet," Chloe replied.

"I could move into your house and help out with chores," Larry said, smiling hopefully at Riley.

Riley smiled. "Uh, thanks for the generous offer, Larry, but no thanks." She turned to the rest of the group. "Why don't we get started? Has anyone come up with any product concepts since this morning?"

"I thought of an idea," Larry said. "You know how people are always losing their keys? What about a key leash—you know, like they have for dogs?"

Riley and the other girls groaned.

"But you could lose the leash," Chloe pointed out.

"Oh. Oh, yeah." Larry scratched his head.

"Besides, we should probably focus on stuff we can sell at school to kids our age," Riley reminded everyone.

"How about mood bubble bath?" Sierra suggested. "The bubbles turn different colors depending on what kind of mood you're in."

Tara cracked up. "Yeah! Red for happy, blue for sad, and purple for when you don't feel like doing your homework." And then she gasped. "Oh, that reminds me!"

She reached into her backpack and pulled out a small purple envelope. On it was a message that read: ENJOY! LOVE, DAD.

"The Crash tickets," Tara announced to Chloe. "Two of them. We're in!"

"Yes!" Chloe screeched. "Oh, thank you, thank you. You are a goddess."

"I aim to please." Tara giggled. She and Chloe exchanged high fives.

Tara turned to the rest of the group. "I'm sorry I couldn't get more," she apologized. "My dad tried, but this was the best he could do. These tickets are rarer than cute, available guys at West Malibu High."

"I'll pretend I didn't hear that," Larry joked. "And don't worry about the concert. I think I'm washing my hair that night anyway."

For the next hour everyone talked about what kind of product they could make for their business. But they couldn't agree on anything serious.

"Okay, this isn't working," Riley said finally. "I think we each need to come up with one *serious* idea that we really believe in by Monday. Then we'll choose a product when we get to class. Okay?"

For the first time, the team agreed.

Well, at least it's a start, Riley thought. And we'll be able to come up with *something* by Monday, right?

chapter three

Chloe's head was still spinning about the Crash tickets when she and Riley got home from the Newsstand.

"Homework," Riley muttered before disappearing upstairs. Chloe wondered what was up with her sister. She shrugged and went off to deliver the magazines to her mother.

Macy was curled up under an afghan on the couch, channel-surfing on the big-screen TV in the living room. She was wearing her navy-blue suit from earlier that day and a pair of fuzzy pink slippers. Her brown hair was held back with a headband.

Chloe noticed a tray of snacks on the coffee table. Way to go, Manuelo! But Macy hadn't touched the fresh fruit, popcorn, or herbal iced tea.

"Hi, sweetie," Macy said without looking up. "You know, this channel-surfing business is terrific! I never had time to watch TV before, so I had no idea how many stations there are!"

Chloe sat next to her mother. "Yeah, well, there *are* a lot. What are you watching?" she asked.

"Well, first I watched the gourmet channel and learned how to make a six-course Thai meal," Macy said. She pointed the remote at the TV set and began clicking furiously through the stations. "And then I watched the American news and then the Canadian news and then the French news and then the South African news. It's amazing how many foreign channels we get! After that I watched the craft channel and learned how to knit scarves out of vegetable-dyed yarns. After *that* I watched five minutes of *Casablanca* and then five minutes of *To Catch a Thief* and then five minutes of *Sabrina* and then five minutes of *Citizen Kane*...."

Click, click, click.

Chloe was getting dizzy as image after image flashed and blurred across the screen. Her mother continued zapping away with the remote as though she were trying to stun an army of *Star Wars* storm troopers with a laser gun.

This had to stop.

Chloe snatched the remote away from her mother and clicked off the TV. "Okay, enough!" she said sternly. "The TV is supposed to *relax* you, not stress you even more."

"I *was* relaxing," Macy insisted.

Chloe handed her mother the pile of magazines. "*These* will relax you," she said. "Here, sit back, munch on some of Manuelo's excellent popcorn, and check out the latest Hollywood divorces."

Macy gasped. "Oh, no!"

"Oh, no, what? Did Reese Witherspoon and Ryan Philippe break up?" Chloe asked.

Macy stabbed a finger at the cover of *Scene* magazine. "This! Shania Tugeau is wearing one of Daisy D.'s dresses!"

[Chloe: Whoops! Big mistake. Daisy D. is one of Mom's major competitors. I think Mom's blood pressure just spiked twenty points.]

"Where is my phone? What time is it in London? I need to call Alessandra at *Scene* immediately." Macy glanced around frantically.

"No way." Chloe reached over and yanked away her mom's magazines. She scanned them quickly and took out anything having to do with fashion, beauty, or style. Too close to business. "Here," she said after a moment. "You can have these back. *Travel Today* and *Fly-fishing Quarterly*. Look, this will relax you—a cover story about fishing for trout in Idaho!"

Macy took the magazines. She started flipping through the pages of *Fly-fishing Quarterly* at breakneck speed. Chloe could hear her muttering under her breath about hemlines and collars and silk crepe.

Chloe grabbed a fistful of popcorn. She had some serious brainstorming to do. Keeping her mother off her feet was not going to be as easy as she'd thought!

Rock music blared inside the Beverly Hills Convention Center as Riley and Jake walked into the trade show on Saturday morning. Riley felt almost dizzy, taking in the frenzied scene: thousands of industry insiders, row after row of booths of fashion accessories, massive TV screens flashing blown-up images of the latest fashion designs. Riley recognized several famous models weaving in and out of the crowd. They were wearing see-through Capri pants, black underwear, tops made of crushed cans and fishnet, and other clothes that seemed *beyond* trendy.

"Well, what do you think, sweetie?" Jake asked Riley.

"It's exciting," Riley said, gazing around the buzzing convention center. "How come *we* don't have a booth?"

Jake frowned. "Good question," he said. "I'm sure your mom had a reason for not setting up one this year. There might be another show in New York that she's gearing up for, I think."

Her father actually sounded nervous. Riley realized that it had been a long time since he'd attended a trade show. He had ditched his usual cutoffs and wrinkled tee for a linen suit and lavender shirt that he had designed. He'd even combed his hair! Riley had almost forgotten how together and businesslike her father could look if he wanted to.

"This is pretty awesome," Riley told him. "Where do we go? What do we do? Just give me orders and I'll do whatever."

"Well, let's check out some of the exhibits. Your mother asked me to take lots and lots of notes." Jake reached into his pocket and fished out a stubby pencil and a crumpled takeout menu from Sushi Palace. "I can write on the back of this. Oh, yes, and I also need to talk to some of her clients," he added. "Grab one of those pink plastic bags over there, honey. They're for loading up on free samples. Your mother will want to see what they're giving away."

Free samples? Excellent! Riley grabbed two bags— one for herself and one for her mother. At the last minute she grabbed a third one for Chloe.

Riley followed her father around as he went from booth to booth, talking to the exhibitors and taking notes. She couldn't believe the freebies—tiny bottles of perfume, cool key chains, earrings, scarves, and more. Her bags were quickly filling up with goodies. It was like Christmas morning without the ugly sweaters from Great-aunt Gertrude!

Riley was stuffing her bags full of lip gloss samples when she realized that her father had disappeared. She glanced around—and saw that he was sitting at a table in the nearby food court. His eyes were closed and he was pinching his nose in a funny way.

Riley rushed up to him. "Dad, what's the matter?

Are you feeling sick?" she asked him, worried. She and Chloe couldn't afford to have *two* parents out of commission!

Jake's eyes fluttered open. "Oh, I'm fine, sweetie. I was just doing a couple of rounds of alternate-nostril breathing. It helps calm me down. I'd forgotten how intense these shows could be."

Riley wrapped an arm around her father's shoulders. "Come on, Dad, let's just hit a few more booths and get out of here. We can go to a café and chill out."

"Good idea, honey. I could use a decaf soy chai latte just about now," Jake said gratefully.

The next exhibit was by a company called Access-Ories. A short woman with spiky blue-black hair was standing behind the booth, unpacking bracelets from a cardboard box. Riley did a double take. The bracelets looked as though they were made out of computer parts!

The woman smiled at Jake. "Jake! What cave have *you* been hiding in? Where's Macy?" she asked him in a friendly voice.

"She's feeling a little under the weather, Zoe," Jake explained. Zoe was about the twentieth person who had asked him that question today. "I'm pinch-hitting for her. She asked me to tell you that she wants to order a hundred of your Ethernet cable belts to go with her new fall line for next year."

"Excellent! Listen, since I'm going to be launching

some hot belts in the spring, is she interested in doing any joint marketing?" Zoe asked. "Also, does she want me to hook her up directly with my distributor? She might shave two, three weeks that way. What's her margin?"

Riley was fascinated as she listened to her father talk shop with Zoe. She had no idea that her mother's work was so complicated! She'd always thought the fashion biz was all about sketching cool designs and hosting a few runway shows. But from what she was hearing, that was just the tip of the iceberg. There was marketing, distribution, down-to-the-wire scheduling, and much, much more.

"I want you to take some of these new bracelets and show them to Macy," Zoe was saying to Jake. "Each one is unique and made almost entirely of used computer parts. It's an artistic expression of the cyber culture we live in. Teenagers are going to be buying them up like mad, both guys and girls. There's a huge unisex market for accessories right now...."

Accessories? Teenagers? Both guys and girls?

That was it! Riley had just figured out the perfect product for their business studies assignment!

chapter
four

Chloe sat cross-legged on her bed with her laptop. She had just clicked SEND on her last E-mail of the morning, when a bell chirped on her computer and an instant message popped up on the screen:

```
TARA-BARA: R U there?
```

Chloe grinned. She was always psyched to get IMs from Tara. She took a quick bite of her bagel with light veggie cream cheese and typed back:

```
CHLOE142: Yes! I'm baby-sitting my mom
today.

TARA-BARA: Keep her away from sharp
objects and fashion TV.
```

CHLOE142: It's not easy. She keeps offering me bribes if I tell her where I hid the remote control and/or her Palm Pilot.

TARA-BARA: Unless she's offering you something major like your own credit card, just say no!

CHLOE142: I'm trying.

TARA-BARA: Keep thinking happy thoughts, like the Crash concert in two weeks!

CHLOE142: Crash rules!

TARA-BARA: I just got their new CD. Come over tonight and we can listen to it.

CHLOE142: No. You'd better come here so we can make sure my mom doesn't try to make a break for the fax machine.

Chloe stopped typing and craned her neck toward the door, listening. She thought she heard a weird noise coming from downstairs. What was her mother up to?

CHLOE142: Gotta go. See U later. xoxo

Chloe logged off, popped the rest of her bagel into her mouth, and ran downstairs.

She found her mom sitting on the couch, wearing the vacation outfit Chloe had picked out for her: stone-washed jeans and a cute vintage T-shirt that said GONE FISHIN'.

Which was all good and fine, except...the television was on, and Macy was taking notes on a legal pad!

Chloe rushed into the living room. "Aha!"

Macy dropped her pen and notebook and stared at Chloe with a guilty expression. "I was just...jotting down some muffin recipes," she said with a weak smile.

Chloe glanced at the TV. A tall, leggy model was strolling down a runway in a red, white, and blue velvet trench coat while a rap version of "New York, New York" throbbed in the background.

Muffins? Chloe didn't think so.

"*Mom*! You know what the doctor said. No work for two weeks!" Chloe grabbed the remote from the coffee table and turned off the TV.

"But I'm so *bored*!" Macy whined. "You won't let me work. You won't let me read fashion magazines. You won't let me watch TV. What am I supposed to do?"

"How about reading? Do you want me to find you a nice book to curl up with?" Chloe suggested brightly. "How about a mystery? Or a juicy celebrity bio?"

"No. I don't feel like reading," Macy grumbled.

Then a brilliant inspiration came to Chloe. "Hey!"

she exclaimed. "I know what would be fun. Why don't we bake cookies?"

"NO! ABSOLUTELY NOT! NO!" Manuelo cried from the kitchen.

> [Chloe: See, it's not that Manuelo has anything against cookies. It's just that the last time I tried to bake something, I kind of set the kitchen on fire. True story—Manuelo has the burned oven mitts and the insurance photos to prove it.]

"Okay, well, how about that massage I suggested?" Chloe said. "Did you call the spa and schedule it for this afternoon?"

Macy shook her head. "I don't feel like a massage, either."

"I'll go with you," Chloe offered. "It'll be a mother-daughter bonding experience."

"No thanks, honey. Maybe another time." Macy sighed.

Chloe was out of ideas. She sat on the couch next to her mom. The two of them stared at the blank TV screen in silence.

Chloe could feel her mother squirming. She could even see her mom's fingers reaching for an invisible remote or cell phone—*anything* to occupy herself with.

This was bad.

Chloe took a deep breath. She was going to have to think of another way to help her mother relax. Otherwise, her mom might have another dizzy spell and land in the hospital. Or, worse, the doctor might tell her mom that she had to take an entire *year* off from work.

"I know!" Macy said suddenly. "Why don't we clean the attic? *That* would be fun."

Cleaning the attic? Fun? "Mom, people don't usually clean their attics when they're on vacation," Chloe pointed out.

"Why not?" Macy said. "I haven't been up there in ages. It will be great to go through all the old things."

Chloe was about to say "No, I have a better idea. Why don't we just hang out at the mall and you can buy me stuff?" But she realized that her mother needed something to do with her hands—something besides signing credit card receipts, that is.

Chloe stood up. "All right, Mom. Lead the way."

"Oh, I forgot we had still this. Look, Chloe, this is the little baby toilet that we potty-trained you on!" Macy exclaimed two hours later.

That is so gross, Chloe thought. Did they really need to go down memory lane about her bathroom habits from zillions of years ago? Still, her mother seemed happy—and almost relaxed—as they rummaged through box after dusty box.

"Oh, and here's a picture of your father and me when we were first dating," Macy said, smiling. Then her smile turned into a frown. "Wow, did I really wear such big shoulder pads? And check out his baggy double-breasted suit! I certainly hope *that* never comes back into fashion."

Chloe snatched the picture away from her. "Work-talk. I'm cutting you off. Next box!"

Macy laughed and reached inside an old wooden crate. She pulled out a black canvas backpack. It was frayed and ripped at the seams.

"I haven't seen this thing in years," Macy murmured. "I carried it around with me all the time when I was in my twenties."

"What did you use it for?" Chloe asked her, curious.

"Oh, for lugging around my sketch pads, my poetry books, my journal…"

Poetry books? A journal? Chloe tried to imagine her mother reading Keats in cafés or writing about her hopes and dreams in a little spiral-bound notebook. It made her smile.

"…and this," Macy said. "I can't believe it's still in my backpack!" She was holding a black-and-silver camera with a large zoom lens. "I used to carry *this* around all the time, too. I was always taking pictures."

"You were into photography?" Chloe asked, surprised. "I didn't know that."

Macy nodded. "I used to love it. At one point I even thought about becoming a photojournalist, but then I decided to go into fashion. And once I started the business, I didn't have time for photography—or for anything else, really."

Chloe thought she detected a hint of wistfulness in her mother's voice. That gave her an idea.

"Mom," Chloe said, "why don't we spend the next two weeks taking photos together? You can teach me how. Wouldn't that be a great vacation activity for us?"

Macy's brown eyes lit up. "Yes, I would love that! What a wonderful idea, honey!" She started rattling off a list. "First we have to go to the camera shop in town and have Mr. Ferguson give this thing a good cleaning and tuning. And we need to buy film—lots and lots of rolls of color and black-and-white, too. Oh, and I wonder what I did with my old German light meter...."

As her mom talked excitedly about taking pictures together, Chloe couldn't help but give herself a mental pat on the back and a silent "Way to go, Chlo!"

Finally she had found an activity that would take her mother's mind off business!

chapter
five

"What a nice morning that was," Macy said as the two of them walked into the house and set their packages and doggie bags down on the kitchen counter. "I haven't had clam strips in ages. They were delicious!"

"I think the secret ingredient is lots and lots of grease." Chloe giggled. She was in an awesome mood. She was making serious progress with Project: Make Mom Take a Vacation.

She and her mom had spent the morning getting the old camera tuned up and buying film—enough to shoot every nook and cranny in Malibu, it seemed. Then they had a long, lazy lunch at a cute little seafood restaurant off the beach. Macy had told her funny stories about her college days as they chowed down on clam strips and French fries.

Chloe rubbed her hands together. "Okay, ready to head out to the beach for my first photography lesson?"

The door banged open and Riley walked in. She was holding three pink shopping bags.

"Hi, honey!" Macy called out. Her eyes zoomed onto the bags. "Are those samples from the trade show? Let me see, let me see."

Oh, no, she's having a relapse, Chloe thought, panicking. "That can wait, Mom. Come on, let's hit the beach!"

But it was too late. Macy had grabbed one of the bags from Riley and dumped the contents onto the kitchen counter. "Hmm, this is cute. This is definitely *not*," she muttered, picking through the stuff. "'Tension.' What kind of silly name is that for a fragrance? Oh, and what's this?"

As Macy continued her survey, Chloe pulled her sister aside and whispered, "I had her just where I wanted her and you ruined it!"

"Sorry," Riley apologized. "I didn't know these bags would set her off like that." She grinned and added, "Listen, though. Guess what? I came up with the perfect idea for our business studies project! See, Dad and I were hanging out at this accessories booth, and—"

"Did you say accessories, Riley?" Macy exclaimed. "What kind did you see at the show? Did the Nouveau Italia people have anything new? What about that bratty little designer Johnny Fast?"

"We were talking about *bike* accessories, Mom, not jewelry and stuff," Chloe fibbed. She grabbed Riley's arm and pulled her into the living room. "Her condition is touch-and-go, Riles. We have to be really careful what we say around her," she whispered.

Riley nodded. "Got it. Anyway, so here's the idea. We should make bracelets! Not just *any* bracelets, but really cool bracelets that guys can wear, too."

Bracelets. Hmm. That made a lot of sense, Chloe thought. They would be pretty easy to make—just a loop of wire or cord or something like that with beads or other accents on it.

And Riley was right. It would appeal to both girls and guys. Chloe's boyfriend, Lennon Porter, liked to wear bracelets. She knew a bunch of other guys who were into them, too.

"I like it," Chloe said. "It's awesome! Let's run it by the rest of the team."

Riley pumped a fist in the air. "A-plus, here we come!"

The doorbell rang.

"I'll get it, Mom!" Chloe called out.

There was no reply from the kitchen. Mom's probably having a feeding frenzy with the free samples, Chloe thought, sighing and crossing the room. It's going to take some serious R and R to undo the damage.

Chloe opened the door. An Overnight Express deliveryman was standing there. "Macy Carlson?" the man said, holding up a package.

Chloe glanced at the return address label. The package was from the *Vogue* magazine offices in New York. It was marked URGENT.

Oh, no, work! Chloe couldn't let her mom see the package or she might go into a stress tailspin.

"I'll sign for it," she said quickly, grabbing the pen from the deliveryman. "Thank you! Good-bye!" She shut the door quickly.

"Who was that?" Macy asked, poking her head through the kitchen doorway.

Chloe hid the package behind her back. "No one. I mean, wrong address. Come on, Mom, get your camera. The light's perfect outside right now!"

"Okay, honey."

As soon as Macy was out of sight, Chloe shoved the package into Riley's hands. "Quick, hide this! I'll distract her," she whispered.

"Why don't I sneak out and take this right to Dad's?" Riley suggested.

Chloe nodded. "Good idea! Go, go, *go*!"

Macy walked into the living room, camera in hand. "Where's Riley going?" she asked. "I wanted to ask her some more questions about the trade show."

"She's, um, going over to Sierra's," Chloe said. "Come on, Mom, let's go play Ansel Adams!"

"I *love* Ansel Adams's photos," Macy said excitedly. "He was an amazing artist. Did I ever tell you about the time I went to see his show in Los Angeles?"

Whew, that was close, Chloe thought as her mother babbled on about the famous nature photographer. *Too* close!

• • •

On Monday morning in business studies, Riley gathered her troops around and shared her new idea.

"Bracelets," Sierra said when Riley had finished explaining about the trade show, about Zoe's Access-Ories booth, about the unisex bracelets made out of computer parts. "Cool!"

"Riley, you are a genius!" Larry gushed. "Bracelets! Who would have ever had such an original idea?"

"It's not *that* original," Tara piped up. "No offense, Riley. It's a good idea, and we should totally go for it, but the trick is going to be coming up with a really unique design."

Riley nodded. Tara was absolutely right. In fact, Riley had spent much of the rest of the weekend doodling different bracelet designs in a sketch pad. Psychedelic bracelets. Glow-in-the-dark bracelets. Flower-power bracelets. ID bracelets with goofy-looking letters. But so far, none of them was quite right.

[Riley: Okay, none of them even remotely resembled a bracelet. When they were handing out the design, sketch, and sew genes, I must have been taking a nap, 'cause I didn't get any.]

"How about a bracelet made out of candy?" Larry suggested.

"It's been done," Sierra replied. "How about a bracelet made from human hair?"

Chloe made a face. "Ewww."

While they brainstormed ideas, Riley scanned the room to check out what the other teams were up to. Blaine the Brain's team seemed to be making cool little bottles of fragrance or lotion or something. Connor Roohan had hooked up with two other cybergeeks and they were designing some sort of computer-related product.

Hmm. Looks like serious competition, Riley thought. She turned her attention back to her team. Everyone was talking at once, sketching, taking notes.

"Can I borrow some paper? My notebook is history," Tara said to no one in particular. She ripped out the last page of her spiral-bound book, tore the dangling wire spiral off, and wrapped it around her wrist a few times.

Chloe handed her several sheets of paper. "Here you go."

"The bracelet has to be easy to do because we'll have to make, like, dozens of them, fast," Sierra said.

"Hey! How about this?" Tara cried out suddenly.

Riley frowned. "How about what?"

Tara pointed to the wire on her wrist. "This. The spiral. We could make bracelets out of notebook spirals!" she exclaimed.

"Yes, yes, yes," Sierra said eagerly. "We could cover them with ribbons or yarn or whatever. Each one would be one-of-a-kind."

"I love it!" Chloe piped up.

"Me, too!" Riley agreed.

"I think my dad has, like, boxes and boxes of old spiral-bound notebooks that he was going to recycle. There's probably thirty or forty bracelets right there," Larry said.

Riley nodded excitedly. The spiral bracelet would not only be cool, it would be easy and cheap to make. "Great teamwork, Tara!" she said.

Tara started sketching like mad. She sketched a spiral with fuzzy yarn wrapped around it. Then she sketched a spiral braided with pipe cleaners. Then she sketched a spiral decorated with bits of mismatched ribbon.

Miss Westmore came down the aisle. "And what has your team come up with?" she asked Riley.

Riley explained the idea of the spiral bracelet.

"Excellent!" Miss Westmore said when Riley finished. "I think it's a terrific concept. Now you can move on to your marketing and production plans."

Marketing. Production. Those words sounded so grown-up and serious. But Riley was psyched and ready to go. She had gotten a crash course in this stuff by following her father around the trade show. She was also supermotivated to learn more. After all, her payoff would be an A-plus!

chapter
six

"**H**ere's a picture Mom took of a seagull going to the bathroom. And, oh, check this out! Here's a picture I took of Mom trying to stand on her head!"

Chloe cracked up as she passed the photos around to the rest of the team. It was after school, and the five of them were sitting around the Carlsons' dining room table. Riley had called a marketing meeting for after school at four o'clock sharp.

"These are awesome," Tara said, glancing through the pile. "Hey, I like this one of you getting knocked down by a wave, Chloe. It's very 'Girl versus Nature.'"

"I've been using photography to help my mom unwind a little," Chloe explained. "It totally works! She's like a different person when she's behind the lens."

"Where's your mom now?" Larry asked her.

"She's in the living room with Tedi. They're playing cards or something," Chloe replied. Tedi was a supermodel and a close friend of the family. Chloe had given Tedi strict orders of no fashion talk with Macy. No necklines. No fabrics. Nothing.

Riley thumped her soda bottle on the table like a gavel.

Startled, Chloe practically dropped her pictures.

"This meeting is called to order," Riley said. "We have to get down to business and focus, focus, *focus*. I don't want to be the voice of doom and gloom, but we're up against some serious competition."

"Bring it on!" Tara cried out. "Our bracelets rule! We're going to win, hands down!"

"*What* competition?" Larry asked worriedly.

"I found out this afternoon that Blaine's team is making little bottles of fruity perfume," Riley replied grimly. "And Connor's team is making an enhanced video game downloading program. *Everyone's* going to want that!"

Chloe frowned. Riley was right. They were going to have to beat out some pretty cool products if they wanted to win.

Then Chloe had an idea. "Hey," she said, "why don't we make some sample bracelets and start wearing them tomorrow? People will notice them and ask us where we got them."

"Excellent suggestion, Chloe!" Riley said, raising her soda bottle in the air.

"Definitely," Tara agreed.

Riley stood up and went off to find some bags of scrap cloth, ribbons, and yarn from her mother's studio. Larry ran next door to get his father's old spiral-bound notebooks. Chloe scavenged around the house for other supplies.

Soon the five of them were busily constructing bracelets. Manuelo brought out a bowl of chips and homemade salsa. Tara put on the new Crash CD she had brought over.

Chloe was pumped. The production line was rolling, Mom was chilling out with Tedi in the living room, and hearing the Crash CD reminded her of the big concert a week from Saturday. Everything was perfect, just perfect....

The phone rang.

"I'll get it!" Chloe said, standing up. She rushed into the kitchen, where the phone was.

Macy rushed in at the same time.

"Mom, I'll get it," Chloe told her.

"No, I'll get it," Macy insisted.

"Macy, where'd you go? I'm about to get gin rummy or whatever," Tedi yelled from the living room.

Macy reached the phone first.

Chloe had to yank it away from her. "Stop that, Mom! Hello?" she said breathlessly.

"Uh, Chloe? Hey, it's me."

"Hey, Lennon," Chloe said, giving her mother an it's-for-me look.

Macy frowned and retreated to the living room.

What's up with that? Chloe wondered. Then she turned her attention back to her boyfriend.

"What are you doing?" Lennon asked her.

"Oh, just hanging with Riley, Tara, Sierra, and Larry. We're working on our business studies project," Chloe explained. "What are you doing?"

"History homework," Lennon replied. "Ask me any question about the Revolutionary War you want. Go ahead, ask me."

Revolutionary War. Hmm. That was the one with George Washington and the British and that tea party in Boston. Chloe wondered if George Washington ever suffered from work-related stress like her mom did.

Another call beeped in just then. "Sorry, Lennon, I have to get that," Chloe said. "It might be my dad."

Chloe pressed the Talk button. "Hello?"

"Oh, hello. Macy Carlson, please," said the person on the other end. "This is Elise at WWD."

"WW-what?" Chloe asked, confused.

"WWD. *Women's Wear Daily*. I have an appointment to do a phone interview with Ms. Carlson at five o'clock Pacific time," Elise explained.

Phone interview? No way! Chloe had to shut this down immediately or her mother would get sucked right back into work mode.

"Um, this isn't really a good time. Could you call back in, um, two weeks?" Chloe asked Elise.

"But I spoke to Ms. Carlson this morning. She said five o'clock would be fine," Elise insisted.

Chloe frowned. Her mother had talked to Elise *today*? How could this have happened? Manuelo had been on keep-Mom-away-from-the-phone duty.

Manuelo walked into the kitchen just then, carrying a bag of groceries. Chloe covered the receiver with one hand. "Manuelo!" she whispered. "This reporter from a fashion magazine says she talked to Mom on the phone—this morning."

Manuelo dropped the grocery bag to the floor and held up his hands. "No! I swear on my stack of enchilada recipes, I watched her like a hawk all day!" he cried out.

Chloe turned her attention back to the phone. "Listen, Elise, something's come up since this morning," she said. "I'm really sorry, but I'm going to have to have Ms. Carlson call you back to reschedule, okay?"

After she said good-bye to Elise, she clicked back to Lennon. "Hey, can I call you back later? I have a mini Mom-crisis on my hands."

Chloe frowned. Obviously her mother had managed to give Manuelo the slip somehow. She was good. *Really* good. This called for drastic measures.

Riley sighed.

Chloe had disappeared to help Tedi baby-sit their mother, saying something about setting up a twenty-four-hour watch system. Tara had gone home to study for an exam. Sierra had taken off for a band rehearsal. Her band, the Wave, was performing in a concert at a local club later this month.

That left just Riley—and Larry.

"So, Riley," Larry said. He leaned across the table and winked at her. "What do you say we take a break from making bracelets and have a romantic dinner together? Maybe on the beach? By candlelight?"

"Uh, no thanks, Larry," Riley said. "Let's make a few more bracelets, then call it a night."

Larry pretended to sniffle. "Oh. Okay. I guess that's a no, then. Another no in a long, long, *long* string of nos..."

Riley rolled her eyes. She and Larry had been doing this for years. He'd ask her out and she'd turn him down. It was sort of a game they played.

"We got a lot done during this meeting," Riley said brightly, trying to change the subject. "We came up with an excellent marketing plan: The five of us are going to wear our bracelets around school for the rest of the week. And we made a few really cool sample bracelets!"

"True," Larry agreed. "If I can't be your boyfriend, Riley, I'll try to be happy being your business partner, your rock, your number one cheerleader. Go, team! Spiral bracelets rule! We're the best! See? I can do it."

Riley heard the kitchen door open and close. A moment later her father walked into the dining room.

"Hi, Dad!" Riley jumped to her feet and gave him a

big hug. "How are you? You look tired! Here, sit down, I'll get you a nice, cold soy shake."

"No, thanks, pumpkin. Hi, Larry," Jake said, waving. "I just came by to see how your mother is doing. Then I have to get right back to work."

"How's it going, Mr. Carlson?" Larry asked him.

Jake rolled his eyes. "Ugh. Don't ask! I have a conference call with Tokyo and Singapore at six. I have a dinner meeting with some clients at seven. I have three press releases to revise tonight. Then I have to get ready for a six A.M. breakfast meeting with our ad agency to talk about marketing for the new resort line."

"Wow. And I thought *we* were busy," Larry said.

"What kind of marketing plans, Dad?" Riley asked.

Jake loosened his tie. "Well, we're doing the usual print ads, of course. We're also hosting simultaneous launch parties in New York, L.A., and Miami and doing a massive Internet blitz. Oh, and I'm in the middle of making a deal with Century Films to feature the clothes in a couple of their upcoming movies...."

Whoa! I'm impressed, Riley thought for the second time in days. Before the trade show she'd always figured that her mother's business was pretty straightforward: someone designed the clothes, some factory sewed the clothes, and then the clothes somehow ended up in hundreds of department stores and cute little boutiques. She'd had no idea that there was so much work to be done *after* the clothes were made.

"Larry," Riley said when her father had disappeared to say hi to Macy. "You know what this means, don't you?"

Larry blinked. "That your dad knows how to do more than sit cross-legged and chant in a foreign language?"

"No! That we're going to have to do more than just wear our bracelets around school if we want to have the number-one business," Riley said. "We have to come up with a really sophisticated marketing campaign, just like Dad was talking about!"

"Does this mean we can have a romantic beach picnic together after all?" Larry asked hopefully.

Riley sighed. "I'll ask Manuelo to nuke some mac and cheese for us. Come on, let's get to work!"

chapter
seven

"**O**kay. I'm handing out a to-do list for the next seven days. Production details are in red. Marketing details are in blue."

It was Tuesday, third-period business studies class. Riley passed out copies of her list to the other members of her team. She had stayed up until midnight last night finishing it—long after Larry had gone home.

She knew she had major dark circles under her eyes, and she couldn't stop yawning. Still, it was worth it. Watching her father in action had convinced her that selling a new fashion product was serious work.

"Um, Riley?" Sierra tossed her hair over her shoulders and frowned at the list. "Under *marketing*? This is a lot to do. I thought we were going to just give away a few bracelets to get people interested."

"That would be way simpler," Tara agreed. "I don't know about the rest of you, but I have two exams to study for this week, which means I'm barely going to have time to brush my teeth, much less do all this." She jabbed an index finger at the list.

Riley sighed. Didn't these people *get* it? "No, no," she said, shaking her head. "Giving away free samples is amateur hour. We need to do everything on this list: fliers in the lockers, an ad in the school newspaper…"

Sierra giggled nervously. "Riley, get real! To get an ad in this week's issue of the newspaper we'd probably have to have it into their office, like, today. Besides, who's going to design the ad? And speaking of design, who's going to design the flier? Me, I can barely draw a stick figure!"

"We would also need to make zillions of copies of the flier," Tara pointed out. "That costs money. Do you really want to spend *money* on a homework assignment? Wouldn't you rather spend it at the mall or whatever?"

No! Riley wanted to shout. I'd rather spend it on this assignment so I can get an A-plus. Instead, she took a deep breath and said, "Look. Trust me. I know what I'm doing here. So are you going to stop arguing and get down to business or what?"

Tara glared at her. "No offense, Riles, but you're acting a little bossy."

"*Way* bossy," Sierra muttered under her breath.

"Hey," Riley said, "somebody's got to take charge."

"Well, who put *you* in charge?" Tara asked.

Riley felt blood rushing to her face. Clearly Tara

didn't care about getting a good grade. If it weren't for Riley, they wouldn't even have a marketing strategy. "What do you mean? My mom and dad are in the fashion business. They taught Chloe and me everything there is to know about marketing! We're practically pros at it!"

Chloe gave Riley a skeptical look.

Okay, so maybe Riley was exaggerating a little. She had to convince the rest of the team that they needed to listen to her.

Larry leaned back in his chair and nodded. "I agree with everything Riley said...whatever it was."

Chloe smiled hopefully at Tara and Sierra. "There *are* some good ideas on Riley's list. We could talk about them, at least."

"I don't think so," Tara said, shaking her head. "The spiral bracelet was *my* idea. Why should I obey Riley's orders?"

"Making bracelets was *my* idea to begin with," Riley shot back. "Besides, I know way more about *selling* them than you do, Tara!"

Sierra held up her hands. "Whoa. Riley, take it easy. It's just a silly bracelet."

Riley glared at Sierra. Was her best friend taking Tara's side on this? She knew how much Riley needed this grade. "What's it to you, Sierra?" she burst out. "You've got an A average in this class. I bet you could care less if we *flunked* this assignment."

"Give me a break!" Sierra cried out.

Larry stood up. "Ladies, ladies, time out!" he said. "Why don't we take five? We can work this thing out."

Tara got up from her chair. "I'm out of here," she said.

"Where are you going?" Chloe asked her.

"The spiral bracelet was my idea. And I'm taking it with me," Tara declared huffily. "I'm forming a new team. Sierra, are you with me?"

"Totally," Sierra said.

"Tara! Sierra!" Riley cried out. "You can't!"

"Just watch us," Tara said, narrowing her eyes. "Larry, are you coming?"

Larry shook his head.

"Chloe, what about you?" Tara asked.

Chloe stared at her. "No way," she said. "You're acting totally stupid!"

Tara shrugged. "Fine! If you think I'm so *stupid*, then maybe I should give your Crash ticket to Sierra. I mean, why would you want to go to a concert with an idiot, right?"

"*What*?" Chloe gasped.

By the time the dust settled, Tara and Sierra had taken their spiral bracelets and gone off to a far corner of the room.

Riley sat there, stunned and silent. For the first time since the beginning of class, she felt a knot of doubt churning inside her stomach like a bad burrito. Were

Tara and Sierra right? Had she been too bossy with her friends?

Larry leaned over and patted her arm. "Don't worry," he reassured her. "We're still the best!"

The best at what? Riley wondered miserably. We just lost two of our team members. And we don't have a product anymore!

chapter eight

"**G**oooooood morning, Malibu! It's going to be a beautiful day: a high of eighty degrees, sunny, and not a cloud in the sky. Coming up at the five o'clock hour we'll be bringing you the latest singles from Junkyard, Pie, and the Sonic Sisters. But first, here's the news...."

Chloe groaned and rubbed her eyes. Did the DJ say "five o'clock hour"? She *had* to be dreaming. Even though it was Wednesday, a school day, there was no way she would have set her alarm clock for a second earlier than seven. Unless...

Chloe bolted straight up. It wasn't just *any* Wednesday. It was the Wednesday that Crash tickets went on sale at the box office!

Last night she had told Lennon about the big fight in business studies and about the fact that she no longer had a Crash ticket. He had suggested that the two of them go to the concert together the old-fashioned way: by getting up at dawn and standing in line for hours and hours to buy tickets.

He had agreed to meet her at the box office at 6:00 A.M. so they could stand in line until eight, when the ticket window opened. That way they could buy tickets, then race over to school by 8:45. It was the perfect plan!

Chloe jumped out of bed and threw on the clothes she had laid out the night before: Capri pants, a red-and-white-striped tee, and turquoise-blue flip-flops. Then she checked the contents of her wallet—fifty dollars in cold, hard cash. Gulp! She'd had to raid her piggy bank, ask for an advance on her allowance, and borrow a ten from Riley on top of that. But it was worth it.

So what if Tara had freaked out on her—over a stupid school project—and given her ticket to Sierra? There was no way Chloe was going to miss the concert. She *had* to be there!

Chloe hooked her backpack over one shoulder and headed downstairs. She grabbed a banana and a yogurt from the kitchen and was about to slip out the back door when she heard a strange noise.

Clickety-clack, click, clickety-clack, click.

Chloe frowned. It sounded like...typing.

She quietly opened the kitchen door and tiptoed into the hallway. The sound was coming from the living room.

There, on the couch, was her mother, typing on her laptop!

"You are so busted, Mom!" Chloe cried out.

Macy's head shot up. "Oh, what, *this*?" she said with a nervous giggle. "I was just...writing in my computer journal."

"How did you find that laptop? I hid it way in the back of the kitchen cabinet behind the canned beets. It was the perfect hiding place!" Chloe walked over and glanced at the screen. "And since when is '*Buon giorno, Signore Armani*' a diary entry?

"I'm a desperate woman, Chloe," Macy admitted, bowing her head.

"Mom, you've got to rest," Chloe said sternly. "I'm taking this away."

Macy sighed. "Oh, all right."

Chloe snapped the laptop shut and stuffed it into her backpack. It was the only way to *really* keep it away from her mom.

But Chloe needed reinforcements. She headed into the kitchen, picked up the phone, and hit one of the speed-dial buttons.

After three rings a sleepy voice answered. "Okay, okay...I'll marry you!"

"Um, Tedi?" Chloe said. "It's Chloe. Did I wake you?"

"I was just having the most awesome dream about Brad Pitt," Tedi mumbled. "Can I go back to sleep? I want to know how it turns out."

"Listen, this is kind of an emergency," Chloe said. "Can you come over right away and hang out with Mom for a few hours? I just caught her writing E-mails to

Milan. Do something to take her mind off business. Take her shopping later. No, that's too close to work. Take her somewhere quiet and force her to be one with nature or whatever."

"All right." Tedi sighed. "Just let me do a quick eucalyptus wake-up facial, grab a latte, and I'll be on my way."

"Thanks, Tedi," Chloe said gratefully. "I knew I could count on you!"

Chloe glanced at her watch as she and Lennon ran through the school parking lot, hand in hand. "It's eight-forty," she said breathlessly. "We're cool."

"I'm sorry about the tickets, Chloe," Lennon said.

[**Chloe**: **Yup, you heard it right. Lennon and I stood in line at the box office for two whole hours. Just when they got to the guy two places in line ahead of us, the box-office lady announced that they'd sold out of tickets. I guess I'm going to miss the concert of the century.**]

At least the morning wasn't a total loss. Chloe had gotten to hang with her boyfriend for two whole hours. They'd even taken goofy pictures of each other with her mom's camera while they were waiting.

"Hey, Tara alert," Lennon said suddenly.

Chloe glanced around. "Where?" And then she saw.

Tara and their other best friend, Quinn Reyes, were standing just outside the front entrance to the school.

Tara and Chloe's eyes met for a second. Then Tara whispered something to Quinn and hurried inside.

Chloe's heart sank. Why was Tara acting like this? Was a stupid school assignment really worth it?

Quinn saw Chloe and Lennon and gave them a little wave. "Hey, Chloe. Hey, Lennon," she called out.

"Hey, Quinn," Chloe replied.

Lennon waved back to Quinn, then stopped to talk to some guy with messy black hair.

Chloe went up to Quinn. "I guess you know what's going on with Tara, Sierra, Riley, and me, huh?"

Quinn squirmed uncomfortably. "Um, yeah. Tara told me."

"I'm sure it'll blow over soon," Chloe said hopefully. "You and I are still okay, right?"

Quinn nodded. "Of course, Chloe!"

Chloe grinned. "That's great! Hey, do you want to go see the new Reese Witherspoon movie on Saturday? I'll buy the popcorn!"

"Um, I can't," Quinn said. "Tara already invited me."

"Oh," Chloe said. She waited for Quinn to say, "Maybe the three of us could go together!" But it didn't happen.

"I've got to go," Quinn said, glancing around. "I promised Tara we'd meet at her locker before class. I'll call you later, okay? I'm really sorry! Maybe we can do something on Friday."

As Quinn walked away, Chloe tried not to feel totally

horrible. She'd lost Tara as a friend. And now she couldn't hang with Tara and Quinn together. All because of some stupid bracelets!

Maybe this dumb fight will be over by Saturday, and the three of us can go see the movie together, Chloe thought.

Or not.

Just then Lennon came up to her. The guy with the black hair trailed behind him. He was wearing superdark shades and a black T-shirt with a picture of a skull on it.

"Chloe, guess what?" Lennon said excitedly. "This is Franco. He's in a couple of my classes. His cousin knows a guy who's selling some Crash tickets."

"Shh, dude, someone will hear us," Franco whispered. "So. You interested?" he asked Chloe.

"Interested? Are you kidding?" Chloe said.

"Cool." Franco glanced to the right and then to the left. He peered at Chloe over the top of his shades. "I'll tell my cousin to tell his contact, okay? I'll let you know the time and place you can meet him. Bring cash."

"I'll go with you, Chloe," Lennon said immediately.

Franco slinked away.

Chloe turned to Lennon and gave him a big hug.

"What was that for?" Lennon said, blushing.

"For setting us up with Crash tickets. You are my hero!" Chloe said happily.

chapter nine

Chloe fanned out her new photos on the living room coffee table. She had just picked them up at the one-hour Qwiklab down the street.

"Check this one out, Riley! Isn't Lennon so cute balancing his backpack on his head? And here's the one of me on my knees, praying for a Crash ticket. I guess the ticket gods weren't listening. Although, did I tell you about this guy Franco? Lennon introduced me to him. He's got this sketchy-sounding cousin who's got this sketchy-sounding friend who's got Crash tickets to sell...."

Chloe stopped babbling. Her sister was obviously not listening. Riley was bent over a notebook, tracing shapes over and over on the open page. She was pressing so hard with her pencil that it looked as though it would snap in half any second.

"Riles? What's up? Do you need some of Manuelo's calming tea?" Chloe asked, concerned.

Riley sighed. "We need a new product to sell—that's what I need. And it's already Wednesday! We are *so* not going to get that A-plus!" She moaned.

"We'll think of something," Chloe reassured her. She frowned and added, "I can't *wait* till this assignment is over. Then maybe Tara and Sierra will start acting, you know, normal again."

Chloe had to admit it, though. Things looked pretty grim right now. Tara and Sierra had barely spoken to her or Riley at school. Chloe had sent Tara a couple of truce E-mails, but Tara hadn't responded. Tara had even ignored one of Chloe's IMs. How much worse could things get?

There was a loud groan from across the living room. Chloe glanced up. Her mother was curled up in a chair by the window, reading one of Manuelo's food magazines, *The Armchair Gourmet*.

"What's the matter, Mom? Are the recipes too complicated?" Chloe teased her.

But Macy wasn't listening. She was muttering to herself. Then she pulled a pen out of her shirt pocket and began scribbling something in the magazine.

Chloe was curious. What was her mother up to?

"Shh," she whispered to Riley, then got up quietly and tiptoed across the room.

Macy was too busy scribbling to notice. Chloe snuck up behind her and took a peek.

There were some papers tucked into the pages of

the cooking magazine. The papers had columns and columns of numbers on them.

Chloe stifled a gasp. Her mother was going over a sales report, conveniently hidden inside *The Armchair Gourmet*!

"Mom!" Chloe cried out. "What are you doing?"

Macy snapped the magazine shut. "What? Oh, nothing. Just reading about, um, different kinds of artichoke dip."

Artichoke dip, my foot! Chloe snatched the magazine away from her mother. "Where did you get that sales report?" she demanded.

"I don't have to tell you!" Macy snapped. "I need to work! Don't you understand? All these leisure magazines and long lunches and massages and relaxation tapes! I feel like I'm in prison!"

Chloe and Riley exchanged a glance. Riley shrugged, as if to say "She's hopeless!"

Chloe sighed. She wasn't ready to give up on her mother—yet. On the other hand, maybe a *little* work wouldn't hurt.

"Okay, Mom," she said finally. "Let's take a break from the sales report. Why don't you come over and sit with Riley and me? You can help us come up with an idea for a new fashion product."

Macy's face lit up. "New product? What sort of new product?" she asked.

"It's a long story," Chloe began.

Macy sat on the couch and listened intently as Chloe and Riley filled her in on their business studies project. When they finished, Macy asked, "What's your target market? Girls? Guys?"

"Both," Chloe said.

"Good," Macy replied. "And what's your production and marketing budget? Probably not a whole lot, huh? But you know, there are some fabulous things you can do with very little money...."

Macy started rattling off ideas, talking a mile a minute. Riley grabbed her notebook and started jotting them down. Chloe stared at her mother in wonder. She was like a kid in a candy store!

Macy paused and glanced at Chloe's photographs, which were still fanned out on the coffee table. "What's this? Chloe, did you take these photos? They're terrific!"

Chloe blushed. "Thanks, Mom!"

Macy picked through the photos, studying each one with an eagle eye. "I like this one of Lennon. Oh, and this one, too." She smiled. "Do you know, when I was your age I used to wear a tiny, tiny photo of my first boyfriend."

"What do you mean, like on a T-shirt?" Riley asked, puzzled.

Macy shook her head. "No, in a locket around my neck. But I guess girls don't wear lockets anymore."

"Hmm, I don't think so," Chloe said. She remembered seeing actresses wearing lockets in a couple of movies. But she couldn't recall any of the girls at school wearing them.

Just then a delicious smell floated into the living room. In the kitchen, Manuelo was cooking Chloe's favorite: beef stroganoff. Chloe glanced at her watch. Mmm, almost time for dinner!

"Chloe!" Riley's voice interrupted her thoughts. "Are you thinking what I'm thinking?"

"Are you thinking about beef stroganoff, too?" Chloe asked, surprised.

"No, silly! Mom just gave us a new idea for our product!" Riley said eagerly.

Macy looked pleased. "I did?"

Riley nodded. "You did! I think our team should make a modern version of the locket. You know, sort of a mini photo album that kids can wear around their necks."

What an awesome idea! "I love it! Picture necklaces!" Chloe cried out.

"Why not call them 'Pic-Laces'?" Macy suggested.

"Mom, you're a genius!" Riley praised her.

And Chloe was glad she had decided to put Macy to work after all.

"Riley, they're playing our song." Larry grinned.

Riley stopped pushing the shopping cart and listened to the tinny music playing over the store speakers. "The Worldmart jingle is our song?" she asked him, confused.

"It is now. Ever since you called me an hour ago and

asked me to come shopping here with you," Larry explained.

Riley laughed. Larry never quit. "Well, I'm glad you're motivated. We've got a lot of shopping to do, and it's already eight o'clock."

"What's on the list?" Larry asked her.

"Well, I didn't exactly have time to make a list," Riley explained. "I was kind of in a hurry to start shopping. I thought we could just, you know, get a bunch of stuff."

"Sounds like a plan to me!" Larry said.

The two of them started down the aisle marked CRAFT SUPPLIES, with Larry singing way off-key along with the Worldmart jingle.

"Morning, noon, or night, we're here to serve you right," Larry sang.

Red yarn. Purple yarn. Plastic and wooden beads. Wire. Riley tossed a few of each item into the cart.

"We've got the lowest prices, our sales team is the nicest...."

Maybe some glitter glue, too. Riley threw in half a dozen tubes.

Wham!

Another cart rammed into Riley's. Startled, Riley looked up to check out who the crazy driver was.

Correction—*two* crazy drivers. Tara and Sierra!

[Riley: **Of all the stores in all of Malibu, they had to walk into this one. There's a line like that in**

the movie *Casablanca*. I heard it when Mom was
channel-surfing the other night.]

"Hey. Trying to eliminate the competition?" Riley
joked.

Tara didn't smile.

Sierra blushed. "Oh, it's you guys," she said. "Sorry
about that."

Riley felt a pang. Sierra would barely look at her.

"Yeah, sorry," Tara said. "What are you guys doing
here?"

"We could ask *you* the same question!" Larry
exclaimed. He stepped in front of Riley and threw his
arms out as if to protect her. Oh, boy.

"Larry, it's cool," Riley said, waving him away. She
glanced at the contents of Tara and Sierra's cart. It was
full of craft supplies, too.

"New product?" Tara said, checking out Riley's cart.

Riley's face lit up. She really wanted to tell Tara and
Sierra about the Pic-Lace. She knew that they, of all people, would appreciate an excellent accessory like that.

"Yeah," Riley said excitedly. "We just came up with
the idea today. It's called the Pic-Lace. It's like a mini
photo album you wear around your—"

"That's nice," Tara interrupted. "By the way, I thought
you'd like to know. The Spiralet is really taking off. We're
on our second round of production!"

"We've given away a ton of them, and everyone
loves them!" Sierra piped up.

"I made some new prototypes," Tara said, holding up her wrist.

Tara was wearing three different spiral bracelets, in green, turquoise, and teal. Riley hated to admit it, but they looked pretty awesome. Tara had wound colored string with tiny silver beads and bells around the wire, making them look even better than the ones the five of them had made together. Tara had also figured out a way to clasp the ends of the spiral together so that the wire ends wouldn't jab the wearer.

"So the point is, we don't *need* to eliminate the competition," Tara bragged. "Our product will do that for us."

Riley felt blood rush to her face. Was this kind of attitude necessary? "Oh, yeah?" she snapped.

"Yeah!"

"Fine!"

"Fine!"

Riley knew she sounded like a five-year-old but she couldn't help it. Tara was being so obnoxious.

"Come on, Larry!" Riley ordered.

Without saying good-bye to Tara and Sierra, Riley did a one-eighty with her shopping cart and started speed walking down the aisle. Larry stumbled behind her.

"They have a lot of nerve," Riley grumbled as she continued down the aisle. "The bracelet was originally *my* idea. And now Tara's acting as if she and Sierra have already won!"

"It's way rude." Larry huffed, trying to keep up with

her. "What can I do? Can I buy you a Worldmart sundae special—ninety-nine cents, two for a dollar seventy-five—to take away your pain?"

Riley shook her head. "We don't need sundaes right now, Larry. What we need is to make some killer Pic-Laces so we can blow Tara and Sierra out of the water!" She was practically shouting.

Larry frowned. "You know I'm with you two hundred percent, O beautiful leader. But I have one itty-bitty question. How do we *make* a Pic-Lace?"

Riley stared at the jumbled pile of craft supplies in her shopping cart. And stared. And stared. In her haste and excitement she had rushed out to buy Pic-Lace supplies without bothering to design the Pic-Lace first.

Riley took a deep breath. "I have no idea!"

chapter
ten

"**I**s this the right address?" Chloe asked Lennon nervously.

"That's what Marcus said," Lennon replied. "Tonight at seven, 425 Surfside Avenue. We're supposed to look for a guy with a red baseball cap. You sure you want to do this, Chloe?" he asked, squeezing her hand. "This morning I thought this was a good idea. Now I'm not so sure. We don't even know this guy."

Chloe took a deep breath and nodded. "Yes, I'm sure. It's our only chance at Crash tickets."

The two of them walked into 425 Surfside—the Time Out Arcade next door to the mall. It was a popular hangout for middle-school kids. Chloe wasn't sure what Marcus's cousin's friend was doing hanging in a place like this.

Oh, well, she thought. Maybe he works here.

The arcade was filled with kids pumping tokens into

video games that pierced the air with sirens, bells, shrieks, and screams.

Chloe glanced around, trying to find a guy in a red baseball cap.

"Over there!" Lennon said. He pointed to someone in the back of the room. Chloe could just make out a red baseball cap beyond a sea of other baseball caps.

She and Lennon wove their way through the crowd to the back of the room. Then they stopped, startled.

The red baseball cap belonged to a short, skinny kid with freckles and braces. He looked like he was maybe eleven or twelve. He was slamming his rail-thin body against a video game and yelling at the top of his lungs, "Come on, go, *go*!"

Chloe and Lennon exchanged a glance. Lennon tapped the kid on the shoulder. "Hey."

The kid turned around, looking annoyed. "Yo, you interrupted my game."

"Uh, Marcus sent us," Lennon said.

"He said to meet you here at seven," Chloe added. She held up her watch and tapped the face of it.

The kid frowned. "Yeah, whatever. You got it?"

"Got what?" Lennon asked him.

"The cash. The hundred-and-fifty bucks."

"*What*?" Chloe practically yelled. "Marcus didn't say anything about a hundred-and-fifty bucks. These tickets originally sold for twenty-five each. That's *fifty* bucks."

"Yeah, well, economics." The kid shrugged. "Do you

want the tickets or not? They're my last two," he said.

What a total brat! Chloe thought. Still, he has something I want. She leaned over to Lennon. "I only have fifty," she whispered. "What do I do?"

Lennon reached for his wallet and took a peek inside. "I've got fifteen. You can have that," he whispered back. "Maybe he'll give us a discount."

Chloe squeezed his arm. "Thanks. You're the best!" She looked up and smiled at the kid. "Would you take sixty-five?" she offered.

The kid smirked. "Get real! You're wasting my time."

Chloe blushed. Maybe she had some change in her wallet. "Sixty-five fifty, and that's my final offer!"

The kid laughed at her and went back to his video game.

[Chloe: Can you believe it? I just got blown off by a kid who's young enough to be my, well, my younger brother!]

"What are you doing, sweetie?" Chloe's mother asked her later that evening.

Chloe turned around. Her mother was standing in the doorway of the bathroom, watching her.

"I'm giving myself a consolation mini-facial," Chloe explained. She smoothed another layer of greenish-brown goop onto her face. "I made it myself out of oatmeal, honey, papaya juice, and avocados."

"Sounds, um, tasty," Macy said. "What's the 'consolation' part for? Is there something wrong?"

"I just lost my last chance for Crash tickets and I needed to cheer myself up," Chloe replied.

Chloe told her mother about her Crash tickets saga, including the fiasco with the miniature scalper. "I wanted to go to that concert more than anything, Mom," she finished sadly. "But now there's no way I'll be able to go."

Macy gave Chloe a hug, carefully avoiding her goopy face. "Oh, sweetie, I'm sorry. If there was any way I could get you tickets, I would."

Chloe noticed that her mother didn't look too happy, either. She had dark circles under her eyes and her forehead was creased with worry.

How selfish could I be? Chloe wondered. Mom is the one who needs TLC, not me!

"Mom, I'm making you a bubble bath. Right this second," Chloe said. "It's going to relax you so much, you'll feel like a piece of overcooked linguine after it's over," she told her cheerfully. "Just give me five minutes. Go get undressed and put on your robe."

"Okay, I guess," Macy said. She headed to her room.

Chloe spent the next five minutes preparing the perfect bubble bath with Dead Sea salts, lavender-scented candles, and a CD of waterfall sounds that her dad had given her. Just for the heck of it, she plucked some daisies from a bouquet in the hallway and let them float around in the water.

I should start my own spa, Chloe told herself proudly as she surveyed the results. "Mom! Your bath is ready!" she called out.

As Chloe trotted downstairs, she heard her mother enter the bathroom and shut the door. Good. If that bath doesn't de-stress her, nothing will, she thought.

Chloe knew that Larry and Riley had gone next door to his house to put together some Pic-Laces that Mom had helped design. Chloe had promised to go over and help out, too—as soon as she'd knocked off her algebra homework, which was due tomorrow.

But just as she'd settled down with her math text-book and a big bowl of strawberries, the phone rang.

Chloe got up to answer it. "Hello?"

"Hey, pumpkin, it's Dad."

Chloe munched on a strawberry. "Hey, Dad, how's it going? How's the wild and crazy world of fashion?" she asked him.

Jake sighed. "We've got a problem, Chloe. I just got off the phone with one of our suppliers. He said that your mom left him a voice mail not two minutes ago! He wasn't sure if he should be dealing with her or with me, so he called me first."

Chloe practically choked on her strawberry. "There's got to be a mistake. Mom's been taking a bath for, like, the last ten minutes!" she said. Then she checked to see if the cordless phone was in its cradle in the kitchen. It was. "I see the cordless, and I hid Mom's cell phone.

How could she have made a business call? And why so late?"

"Well, I can't explain it, but I'm worried," Jake said.

"Let me call you back in a second, Dad, okay?" Chloe hung up and went up the stairs. There *had* to be an explanation!

Once upstairs Chloe could hear the faint sound of her mother's voice coming from the bathroom. She tiptoed up to the door and pressed her ear against it.

"Uh-huh. Roberto, we definitely need that shipment by the end of the month," her mother was saying. "I'm sorry, can you hold on? I've got another call coming in."

Chloe held in a gasp. Her mother was talking business with someone—on the phone! But how? Mom's cell was hidden in a deep, dark corner behind some smelly old sneakers in Riley's closet.

The bathroom door was open a crack. Chloe angled her head just so and peeked inside.

Her mother was sitting on the edge the bathtub, still dressed in her robe. She had a blue cell cradled under one ear.

She had never even gotten into the bath!

And the blue cell phone was not hers. Mom's cell was silver.

First the sales report that appeared mysteriously in Macy's clutches. Now the blue mystery phone. Where is mom getting all this stuff? Chloe wondered.

chapter
eleven

[<u>Riley</u>: Finally, after everything we've been through, we have a product! Okay, so it took almost a week, and I'm not speaking to two of my closest friends because of it, and I feel almost as stressed as Mom. But, hey, it's business, right? And I'm THIS MUCH closer to that A-plus.]

It was Thursday, and Riley had come into school early after being up till midnight. She, Chloe, and Larry were planning to stuff Pic-Lace fliers into every single student locker. Larry was off making copies of the flier she'd created last night.

Standing in the empty hallway, Riley studied the Pic-Lace prototype hanging around her neck. The design had been partly her mom's idea, and Macy had helped put it together. The tiny frame for the Pic-Lace was made out of sculpted wire with little beads glued to it. There was an opening at the top of frame for the photo to slide into and stay securely in place. The frame then hung from a piece of braided leather cord that tied around the neck and could be adjusted to different lengths, depending on what mood you were in.

"Riley, here they are, hot off the presses!" Larry came running up to her, holding a big stack of hot-pink fliers. He shoved one of the fliers in front of her face.

Riley nodded, pleased. It looked perfect!

In the middle of the page were pictures of Pic-Laces, artistically angled. Arrows pointed to the centers of the frames, with the words HIS/HER PICTURE HERE!

Riley punched Larry in the arm. "Good work, Slotnick!"

Larry smiled dreamily and touched his arm. "I'm never washing that arm again. Ever."

"Okay, Larry. We've got forty-five minutes till home-room," Riley said, glancing at her watch. "Why don't you take a bunch of these and stuff the lockers in the main hallway? I'll cover this hallway. And I'll give a bunch to Chloe, too. She should be here in five minutes. She had to hide all of Mom's work stuff first."

"Got it," Larry said. "We've got a winner, baby!" He pumped a fist in the air. Then he disappeared down the hall.

Riley giggled. Then she got down to business. She had lots of locker stuffing to do in a really short amount of time.

Wham!

Someone bumped into her from behind. "Oh, I'm so—" the person began.

Riley whirled around. Sierra was standing there. She was dressed in a long black skirt, a lacy black vintage top, and dark shades.

"Oh, Riley, hey," Sierra said awkwardly. She took her glasses off and stuck them into her backpack. Riley noticed that she was wearing two black and blue Spiralets on each wrist.

"We seem to be doing this a lot," Riley joked. "You know, slamming into each other in public places. Maybe we should both get accident insurance or something."

Usually Sierra would have laughed at Riley's dumb joke. But today she didn't even crack a smile. Instead, she gave a little cough and looked away.

"Well, I've got to run and meet Tara," Sierra said. "By the way, have you seen our ad?"

Riley shook her head. "What ad?"

Sierra reached into her backpack and pulled out the school paper. It was an early copy of the end-of-the-week issue.

Sierra turned to the last page. There was a full-page ad for the Spiralet!

Riley studied the ad closely. Wasn't it Sierra who had said they didn't have time to make a newspaper ad when they were a team? But that didn't really matter anymore, did it?

And she had to admit, the ad looked really cool.

Way cooler than their Pic-Lace flier, which suddenly seemed amateurish by comparison.

"It's totally great," Riley told her. She didn't feel like acting catty and competitive with her best friend.

"Thanks." Sierra shrugged. "Anyway, I've got go. Tara's waiting for me. We have to…um, do some stuff."

As Sierra walked away Riley felt a sharp pang in her heart. She wanted to call out after her, as she always did: "Talk to you later! Hey, you want to hang out after school? Rollerblade on the beach? Give each other pedicures?"

But she couldn't get the words out of her mouth.

Chloe walked into the house after school, her arms aching from lugging a huge, heavy box she'd brought from Mr. Ferguson's shop. She set it down on the floor with a loud *thunk*.

She couldn't wait to surprise her mother!

"Mom!" she called out.

No answer.

Manuelo poked his head out of the kitchen. "Your mother has been in her room all day. I just made some fresh guacamole. Do you want some?"

Chloe frowned. "In her room all day? Is she okay?" she asked.

Manuelo shrugged. "She said she was tired and wanted to be left alone. It's fine. It is good for her to nap. It will make the little thinking cells in her brain feel better."

"Save some of that guacamole for me, please," Chloe

said, then trotted up the stairs. Her mother's bedroom door was open. Chloe knocked softly and walked in. "Mom?"

Macy was sitting cross-legged on her bed. As soon as she saw Chloe, she shoved something under her pillow. "Oh, hi, honey. Did you just get home?" she asked, giggling nervously.

Chloe frowned. Her mom was dressed in jeans and a white blouse, and she looked totally awake—not as if she'd been napping at all.

"Mom? What did you just put under your pillow?" Chloe asked her.

"What? Oh—nothing." Macy said.

"Right," Chloe said. She headed over to the pillow and stuck her hand underneath. And pulled out…

A sketch pad!

The pad was brand new. In fact, it had a cash receipt from the art supply store stuck in the flap, dated today. Chloe flipped through the pages. There were dozens of sketches in charcoal and pen: dresses, swimwear, gowns, and more.

"You've been working again," Chloe said. "You know you're not supposed to do that. And where did you get this sketch pad? Manuelo said you haven't been out all day."

"I don't have to answer that question," Macy replied. "Besides, this isn't work. It's art!"

Chloe sighed. Her mother never quit.

Chloe thought about the surprise she had brought home. Maybe, just maybe, it might do the trick and take Mom's mind off work. At least for a few minutes, anyway.

"I want to show you something, Mom," Chloe said. "Come with me."

"What is it?" Macy asked, suspicious.

Chloe grabbed her mother's hand. "Just trust me, okay?" She led her mother downstairs. Then she picked up the heavy box she'd brought home and carried it into a small storage room in the back of the house.

"What are we doing?" Macy asked her. "What on earth is in that box? Don't tell me it's more fishing magazines!"

Chloe opened the box and started pulling out various supplies, including large pieces of black cloth and jugs of developing chemicals. "Ta-da!" she announced. "Dad and I went to get you everything you need to make a mini darkroom!"

Macy's face lit up. "Really? Oh, Chloe, how wonderful! I haven't used a darkroom in about twenty years!"

Chloe grinned. "Well, let's get started!"

They got to work. Chloe brought in her boom box and put on a Beatles CD. Macy turned it up full blast, singing along and swinging her hips as she dug into the box of equipment.

The two of them spent the next hour setting up the space. Maybe it was longer than that—Chloe wasn't sure. They were having such an awesome time.

[Chloe: Check out my mom! She's having a blast, and she's doing it without a cell phone or computer or pager or anything. She's freed herself of her dependence on office equipment. And do you know what? She's a lot of fun when she's like this!]

Riley drummed her fingers on the table at lunch. It was Friday, and the school cafeteria was crammed with students chowing down on veggie burgers and gabbing about their weekend plans.

At the next table some of the students were talking about Connor Roohan's computer-download program. A few of them were wearing Spiralets, too.

When are the announcements going to come on? she wondered anxiously. Lunch will be over in fifteen minutes!

Then the speakers crackled, and the principal's voice came on. "Good afternoon, students. I have a quick announcement to make."

Much to Riley's distress, the kids in the cafeteria kept on gabbing. She could barely hear the principal's words.

"...next Wednesday at two P.M.," the principal was saying—something about a meeting or pep rally or whatever. "And now here's a little something from Chloe Carlson and Larry Slotnick."

Yes! Riley thought. She sat up and crossed her fingers under the table.

A moment later Larry's and Chloe's voices rang over the speakers:

"You want to carry her photo around, but it's way too big and clunky…." Larry sang. "Well, here's a way to do just that, and also look real funky…."

"You want to carry his photo around, 'cause he's cute and sweet and true…." Chloe sang. "Well, here's a way to do just that and score some style points, too!"

Then Larry and Chloe both sang: "Pic-Lace, Pic-Lace, Piiiiic-Lace—it's cool and it's homemade…Pic-Lace, Pic-Lace, Piiiiic-Lace—buy one in every shade!"

Everyone in the cafeteria cracked up and broke into applause.

Riley smiled. Yes! The Pic-Lace jingle, which the three of them had written late last night, was a major success. It *had* to beat Tara and Sierra's ad in the school paper!

The cafeteria suddenly went dark. What's going on? Riley wondered.

The other students started whispering. "Hey, is this supposed to make the food taste better?" someone yelled out.

On one wall of the room a large-screen TV glowed to life. Sierra's image filled the screen. She was dressed in a skintight strapless red dress and matching boots, and she was strumming on her guitar. She started singing a song about the Spiralet!

Riley watched, feeling both mesmerized and miserable. The camera alternated between wide shots that showed Sierra jamming and close shots that focused on the many Spiralets on her wrists. The video was incredible. In just seconds the entire cafeteria was rocking and cheering and singing along.

This is bad, Riley thought. This is really, really bad.

Between Sierra's cool, music-video-type ad and the buzz about Connor's computer download, did the poor Pic-Lace stand a chance?

chapter
twelve

"We're doomed." Chloe groaned.

"Totally doomed," Riley agreed.

"I thought our jingle ruled, if do I say so myself," Larry said.

Chloe picked at her pizza. Even though it had extra garlic, just the way she liked it, it wasn't managing to cheer her up. It was Friday night, and the three of them were meeting at Chloe and Riley's house to make the rest of the Pic-Laces as well as figure out some last-minute marketing plans.

They were supposed to set up their Pic-Lace booth on Monday, so it was crunch time. They had ordered in pizza and spread out on the living room floor with tons of supplies. Chloe's favorite radio station, WMBU, was jamming in the background.

Despite the high-energy atmosphere, though, it was hard to get any work done. There was too much to be upset about. Sierra and Tara's video. Sierra and Tara themselves, who were still acting totally cold to both Chloe and Riley. And last but not least, the fact that Chloe would not—repeat, *not*—be sitting in the audience of the Crash concert a week from tomorrow...

Riley took a swig of her soda. "I wonder what Sierra and Tara are doing right now," she said.

"Probably hiring an airplane to write *Buy Spiralets* across the sky," Chloe joked.

"I miss them," Riley said wistfully.

"I do, too," Chloe admitted.

The two of them sighed.

"Ladies, ladies!" Larry slammed a hand down on the coffee table. "Ow! I mean, cheer up! Let's focus! We have an awesome product. All we have to do is convince people to buy it."

"That's true," Chloe said. She was glad *one* of them was motivated.

"Does anyone have any marketing strategies we could try over the weekend? How about a Web site? Or a massive E-mailing campaign?" Larry said.

Riley nodded slowly. "How about a buy-one-get-one-free offer?" she suggested.

"Yes! Or we could start a club. Club Pic-Lace. Every time you buy three Pic-Laces, you get something free," Larry added.

"Or we could have free munchies and drinks at our booth," Chloe said. "Maybe Manuelo could help us make them!"

"Manuelo could make what?" Manuelo said, passing through the living room. "Whatever it is, it must be very simple. I am very exhausted from keeping Miss Macy away from the phone all week."

"How is Mom, anyway?" Riley asked Chloe.

Chloe shrugged. "So-so. When we're taking photos or working in the darkroom together, she's totally laid back. But as soon as I turn my back, she manages to get her hands on work. I don't know where she's getting all of it. *Someone* must be smuggling her reports and cell phones and stuff."

Manuelo frowned. "Don't look at me! I am no traitor!"

"*Listen*, you guys!" Larry was on his feet, pointing frantically at the radio.

"What is it, Larry? Is your favorite song on or something?" Riley teased him.

Larry shook his head. "No, no, no! Contest. Crash. *Tickets*!" he sputtered excitedly.

Chloe's ears perked up. "What did you say about Crash tickets?"

Larry held a finger to his lips. "Shh!"

The DJ's voice came over the radio: "WMBU is having a call-in contest to celebrate our fifth anniversary on the air. The winner will get five Crash tickets! That's right, five! Call now, and if you're the fifteenth caller..." Her voice faded away as a Crash song, "Always True," faded in.

Chloe couldn't believe it. It was the miracle she needed! Another chance to score Crash tickets!

And not just one Crash ticket—*five* Crash tickets. She could take her friends! Except for Tara and Sierra, that is, who weren't really acting like her friends these days, anyway. Besides, they already *had* tickets.

Chloe ran into the kitchen and grabbed the phone. Macy's voice came over the receiver.

"Uh-huh, Marcel, and how many of those can you get me by next Friday?" she was saying.

Chloe gasped. Macy was on the other extension, sneaking in an illegal work call, but Chloe needed the phone! "Mom, get off the phone, now!" she cried.

"Oops, Marcel, my other line's beeping, got to call you back," Macy said, hanging up quickly.

"It's 555-WMBU," Larry called out from the living room. "Go, Chloe, *go*!"

Chloe punched in the phone number. Busy signal. She hung up and hit Redial. Another busy signal!

She continued hanging up and hitting Redial. On the tenth try, she got through. Yes!

"Hello, this is WMBU. Who's this?" a woman's voice said. It was the WMBU DJ, Maxine!

I'm in! *I'm going to the Crash concert*! Chloe's knees felt weak.

"Hello? Are you there?" Maxine asked.

"Uh, I'm here. This is Chloe, from Malibu."

"Hey, Chloe-from-Malibu, you're our lucky fifteenth caller. Are you ready to answer our quiz questions?" Maxine asked her.

Quiz questions? Nobody had said anything about a test. Chloe frowned at Larry and Riley, who were standing in the doorway. Larry was nodding his head like mad and mouthing the words, *Say yes!*

"Yes," Chloe said automatically.

"Great! Here's your first question, Chloe. What is the last line of Pie's first hit single, 'Get Out Of My Head'?"

I know that one! Chloe thought excitedly. "'If you don't get out of my head, then I will,'" she replied.

Larry and Riley both grinned and pumped their fists in the air. Chloe grinned back, her heart racing like mad.

"You got it, Chloe!" Maxine exclaimed. "Now for your second question. What is rocker Jansen's real name? I'll give you a little hint—his first name is Bartholomew."

Jansen's *real* name? Chloe thought that *was* his real name. And what kind of first name was Bartholomew?

Chloe felt her palms growing sweaty as the seconds ticked away. She did a mental inventory of all the back issues of her music magazines. Jansen. Bartholomew. Nothing was coming to her.

"We're running out of time, Chloe," Maxine said.

Just then Chloe realized that Larry was motioning at her. He flopped down on the kitchen floor and began wriggling. He was giving her a hint!

Chloe tried to guess what he was. He was a snake. No. He was a crazy person. Yes…no. He was a…

And then it came to her. "Fish!" she cried out. "Bartholomew Fish!"

"Yes!" Maxine screeched. "You got it, Chloe-from-Malibu!"

Chloe clamped a hand over her mouth to keep from screaming. The tickets! She had won the Crash tickets! Riley and Larry were clapping and jumping up and down.

"Now you just need to answer one more question to get you there," Maxine said.

Riley and Larry stopped clapping and jumping.

Chloe's mouth dropped open. "One...m-m-more?" she sputtered.

"That's right, Chloe-from-Malibu," the DJ said. "As soon as we get off the line, please give our producer, T-Bone, your phone number. Be at that number on Tuesday at four o'clock. We'll pick one question from the many that our listeners have been E-mailing us. And you know what happens if you get it right, right?"

You bet I do, Chloe thought. "Four of my friends and I are going to hear Crash live!" she cried.

It was late, almost eleven. Chloe, Macy, and Manuelo had all gone to bed, and Larry had gone home.

Riley was wide awake, though. She was sitting in the dining room, arranging and rearranging a bunch of Pic-Laces. They look good, she thought. Actually, they look *fantastic*.

But were they fantastic enough to beat Tara and Sierra? Or Connor's team? Or Blaine the Brain's team, for that matter?

She heard a soft knock on the door. Who could it be? Had Larry forgotten something?

Riley got up and peeked out the window. Her father was standing on the porch. Next to him was a bald man dressed in a black suit and funky-looking red tie.

Who was the bald guy? And what was her dad doing here so late?

Riley opened the front door. "Dad?" she said in a soft voice so as not to wake anyone. "What's up?"

"Sorry, Riley," Jake apologized, stepping inside. "I know it's late. This is Max Vong. Max, this is my daughter Riley. We just had a dinner meeting, and Max wanted to see one of your mother's portfolios immediately," he explained. "I thought I could just come by and sneak one out of here without disturbing her."

Riley stared at the bald man. Max Vong! Everyone knew who Max Vong was. He was the founder of Vong, a chain of small, trendy designer boutiques all over the West Coast.

"*Fabulous* to meet you!" Max said, shaking Riley's hand.

Riley smiled. "Um, fabulous to meet you, too."

"Is your mom upstairs?" Jake asked Riley.

Riley nodded. "Yes, it's safe—I mean, she's asleep."

Jake smiled nervously and nodded. "Good. Max, make yourself comfortable. I'm just going to go find that portfolio."

"Fabulous!" Max exclaimed.

Jake headed for Macy's studio. Left alone with Max, Riley wasn't sure what to do. Should she offer him coffee? A cookie? Give him a tour of the house?

"So, you're one of Jake and Macy's daughters," Max said. "That's fabulous! Are you going to be a fashion designer when you grow up?"

Riley blushed and shrugged. "I don't know. Mom and Dad are way more talented than I am."

"They are very talented, indeed. That's why we're so eager to get their designs into Vong." Max wandered into the dining room, and his gaze fell on the row of Pic-Laces on the table. "What are these?" he asked Riley. "They're fabulous!"

Fabulous? Did he really say the Pic-Laces were fabulous? Riley's head was spinning.

"They're, um, Pic-Laces," Riley explained. "My friends and I are making them for our business studies class. Our teacher asked us to create a product and market it. Whoever has the best-selling one gets the best grade. So we came up with this idea to do a modern-day version of the locket. You can put a picture of your boyfriend or girlfriend in it or whatever...."

Riley's voice trailed off. She was babbling like a crazy person. What did a big executive like Max Vong care about her business studies class, anyway?

Max picked up a couple of the Pic-Laces and studied them carefully. "You know, we've been thinking about expanding into the teen market at a few of our

Vong stores. These Pic-Laces would be just right. Can you fill an order for us?"

Riley gaped at him. "You want an order? Of Pic-Laces? For your stores? For real?"

Max laughed. "For real. Can you manage a small order by next Wednesday?"

Riley couldn't believe it. Max Vong was interested in their Pic-Laces! She couldn't wait to tell Chloe and Larry!

"Next Wednesday? No problem," she told Max.

Max grinned. "Fabulous!"

chapter thirteen

On Monday morning the main hallway of West Malibu High was jammed with booths and sales displays. Riley finished tacking up Chloe's Pic-Lace photos, which she'd blown up into posters, and stood back to admire her work. Perfect!

Larry leaned back in a folding chair and put his feet up on the display table. "Yup. Yes, sir. I figure that with this Max Vong deal, we've got that A-plus sewn up." He cupped his hands over his mouth and yelled, "In case anyone didn't hear, that was Max Vong. M-A-X V-O-N-G."

"What's the deal with Max Vong?" Tara called out from the next booth.

Riley glanced over. Tara and Sierra had been assigned a booth right next to theirs. They had created a cool tree sculpture out of wire and dried leaves to display their Spiralets. They hadn't said one word to Riley, Chloe, or Larry all morning—until now.

"Max Vong asked us for an order of Pic-Laces for his

stores," Riley said, smiling triumphantly. "Isn't that the coolest?"

"Oh," Tara mumbled. She couldn't seem to muster one of her usual funny comebacks. "That's, um, great."

"Yeah," Sierra said. "Congratulations."

Riley had been bursting to tell Tara and Sierra the big news all weekend, but telling them didn't make her as happy as she'd thought it would. In fact, she felt kind of bad, especially since Tara and Sierra suddenly looked miserable.

[Riley: You're probably thinking, this girl has a major deal with Max Vong and she's moping? Could she be more ungrateful? The thing is, what fun is it being a mega business success when your best friends are barely speaking to you? Besides, we may be doing well out in the real world but here at the West Malibu High business studies booths, we're sinking. We've only sold two Pic-Laces. I think Tara and Sierra have sold a total of three Spiralets. Connor Roohan and his cybergeek buds, on the other hand, are raking it in with their video game downloading program.]

A girl came by their booth, looked at a Pic-Lace, and moved on to Connor's booth. She got in line behind a dozen other students.

"We still have a few more days to sell these things," Chloe said.

Riley nodded grimly. Maybe, just maybe, things would turn around by then.

"This is a picture of Tedi jogging on the beach. This is Tedi talking on the phone. This is Tedi trying to make me a cappuccino. As you can see, she wasn't used to our espresso maker and the foam kind of exploded."

Chloe leaned forward on the couch. She nodded and smiled as Macy showed her photo after photo of their supermodel friend. Tedi had spent the day at the Carlsons' house, and Macy had shot dozens of rolls of her just for fun.

Chloe flipped though the photos. Her mother was an amazing photographer. Even with everyday subjects, like Tedi talking on the phone, Macy managed to capture just the right combination of light and shadow as well as interesting little details.

Chloe stared at a picture and narrowed her eyes.

Interesting little details...like the fact that Tedi was talking on a *blue* cell phone. The same color phone Chloe had caught her mom using to make a business call!

"Uh, Mom?" Chloe said slowly. "Tedi's cell. It looks kind of familiar."

Macy blushed and grabbed the photos from Chloe. "What? Oh, that. Well, I'm sure you've seen her talking on it before. So, what would you like for dinner?" she added brightly. "I could microwave one of Manuelo's Meals in a Minute. Or would you prefer a salad?"

"Mom, we already ate dinner," Chloe reminded her. Why was her mother acting so weird suddenly?

Just then the doorbell rang. "I'll get it!" Macy said, leaping to her feet.

Chloe stood up, too. "I'll get it!"

The two raced to the door. Macy reached it first.

It was Tedi. "Uh, hey," she said, glancing nervously from Macy to Chloe to Macy again. "How are you guys doing tonight?"

"Hi, Tedi," Macy said. "Chloe was just, uh, leaving. She has homework to do, don't you, honey?"

Chloe shook her head. "I'm *done* with my homework, Mom."

"You are? Oh, well, good for you, sweetie." Macy turned to Tedi. "So, Tedi, do you have that...*scarf* I let you borrow?" she asked her.

Tedi frowned. "Scarf?"

Macy glared at her.

"Oh, *that* scarf," Tedi said brightly. She reached into her purse and pulled out a manila envelope.

Chloe stared at the package and frowned. Scarf? I don't think so. Something really, really fishy is going on!

Before Tedi could hand the envelope to Macy, Chloe grabbed it and ripped it open.

"No!" Tedi and Macy shouted at the same time.

Chloe peered into the envelope. Inside were the latest issues of *Women's Wear Daily* and *Vogue*, along with some fabric swatches.

"Tedi, it was you!" Chloe exclaimed. *"You're* the one who's been smuggling work to Mom. The cell phone, the sales report—and now this!"

"Don't blame Tedi. It was all my fault!" Macy cried. "I begged her to bring me those things. I was going crazy!"

Chloe sighed. "Mom, you know what Dr. Schynoll said. And, Tedi, you should have known better!"

"Your mother bribed me with a new pair of Manolo sandals," Tedi said, shrugging. "Call me easy, but I'll do just about anything for a new pair of Manolos."

The phone rang.

Macy made a mad dash for it. "I'll get it!"

"No, I'*ll* get it!" Chloe said, racing after her.

Macy reached it first and picked it up. "Hello?" she said breathlessly. "Yes, this is Ms. Carlson."

Oh, great, a work call, Chloe thought in frustration. Mom is right back to full throttle!

"Uh-huh," Macy was saying to the person on the other end of the phone. "You want how many? Of what? By when? I see. Uh-huh. Excuse me just a sec."

Macy covered the receiver with one hand. "Um, Chloe?" she said, sounding confused. "I think this call is for you or your sister. It's someone from Max Vong's office, and she says he needs two hundred Pic-Laces delivered by Wednesday morning."

Chloe felt all the blood drain out of her face.

Two *hundred* Pic-Laces? By *Wednesday morning*?

How were they ever going to do that?

chapter
fourteen

"Twenty down, one hundred and eighty to go," Larry groaned. "My hands are killing me. Does anyone want to massage them? Any volunteers? Riley?"

It was Tuesday morning. Riley, Larry, and Chloe were hanging out at their booth, still frantically assembling Pic-Laces for the Max Vong order.

Riley felt guilty about putting Larry and Chloe through this. When Max Vong had asked her to fill a *small* order last Friday, she'd thought he meant, like, maybe twenty—thirty, tops. She had no idea he was thinking two hundred!

Note to self, she thought. When making a business deal, hammer out the details up front.

Despite everything, though, she was glad for the huge order. Business was still slow at their booth. Between yesterday and today they had sold only six Pic-Laces, total.

She sneaked a peek at Tara and Sierra's booth. She

knew they weren't doing too well, either. On top of all that, Tara and Sierra were kind of talking to them now. But the competition between the two booths was making it really hard to make up.

Riley wished that they could just put the whole thing behind them. She wanted her friends back—and she wanted them back now.

"Hi, do you have one in purple?"

Riley looked up. A girl from her history class—Maddie something—was standing in front of their booth. She was wearing a purple Spiralet on one wrist. "I want a Pic-Lace to match this," she explained.

Larry smiled. "Great idea! Here, I've got the perfect one for you right over here." He held up a Pic-Lace with purple beads around the frame.

A girl with curly red hair came up behind Maddie. "What'd you buy, girlfriend?" she asked her.

Maddie grinned. "Hey, Elle. I'm getting a Pic-Lace to match my Spiralet," she replied.

Elle nodded approvingly. "Cool! Maybe I'll get one of each, too. In red!"

Riley sat up. Was it her imagination, or was a new trend being born right before their eyes? Pic-Laces and Spiralets. Spiralets and Pic-Laces...

"Riles!"

Riley glanced over at the Spiralet booth. Could it be? It was! Sierra was calling out her name—and smiling!

"Are you thinking what I'm thinking?" Sierra said.

Pic-Laces and Spiralets. Spiralets and Pic-Laces. A winning combination—just like the friends who had created them. Riley smiled back and nodded. "Definitely!" she replied.

"Here's your change. Thank you, and tell all your friends about Inseparables!"

Chloe handed the guy fifty cents along with his purchase: a green Spiralet and a green Pic-Lace. She, Riley, Larry, Tara, and Sierra had pushed their two booths together, paired up their accessories according to color, and renamed the combination Inseparables.

After only an hour both teams had almost sold out of their stock. The Inseparables were a huge success!

"Okay, I'll be the first one to say it," Tara said as she counted the money in their cash box. "This team never should have broken up. I'm sorry I was such a jerk!"

"I'm sorry I was such a jerk!" Chloe said.

"No, I was the jerk!" Riley said.

"Me, too!" Sierra piped up.

Larry pretended to wipe away a tear. "This is so beautiful, you're all going to make me cry."

Chloe put a hand on Tara's arm and drew her aside. "I am so sorry we got into a fight over a bunch of bracelets," she said in a low voice.

"Me, too. I've really missed you, Chloe!" Tara said, giving her a hug.

"I've missed you, too!" Chloe said, hugging back.

Tara pulled away and frowned. "And I feel really bad about the Crash ticket. I don't know what to do now. I already promised it to Sierra."

"Don't worry about it. I still have a chance to go," Chloe replied. She told Tara about the radio contest. "The station is calling me at four today. If I get the question right, I'll get to go to the Crash concert!"

"But what if you don't?" Tara said worriedly. And then her eyes lit up. "I know! Why don't you take my ticket, and you and Sierra can go?"

Chloe shook her head. "That's really sweet, Tara. But I want to try to win that contest. That way we can *all* go."

"What's this?" Miss Westmore said, coming up to their booth. She glanced around. "What happened to the two booths?"

"Business merger!" Larry announced. "Ta-da!"

"The Pic-Laces weren't selling too well, and neither were the Spiralets," Riley explained. "So we decided to sell them together and rename the product. Now kids are buying them like crazy!"

Chloe also told Miss Westmore about the Max Vong deal. And then something occurred to her—something major.

"Hey!" Chloe said to her teammates. "Maybe we can convince Max Vong to sell the Spiralets together with the Pic-Laces, too!"

Tara and Sierra's jaws dropped.

"No way! For real?" Tara cried out.

Chloe grinned and shrugged. "We can talk to him about it. If we're lucky, he'll think it's a *fabulous* idea and go for it."

Miss Westmore gave the team—the new and improved team—a great big smile. Her smile was so big, in fact, that Chloe could practically see her tonsils.

"This merger is really commendable," Miss Westmore gushed. "If you keep going like this, your team is sure to win and get an A-plus!"

Riley grabbed Chloe's hand and squeezed.

Chloe squeezed back. Everything is finally working out! she thought. Now if only I can win those Crash tickets!

"Riley, turn your face a little to the left. Sierra, get closer to her. Hold up those bracelets, girls. Okay, smile!"

Click!

Chloe watched as her mom took a bunch of photos of Riley and Sierra together. The two of them were modeling the Inseparables.

It was after school on Tuesday, and the team had gathered at the Carlsons' house to make the rest of the Pic-Laces for the Max Vong order. Macy had offered to take photos of the Pic-Laces and Spiralets together in order to pitch the Inseparables concept to Max Vong.

"I am so proud of you girls," Macy said excitedly as she snapped away. "Oh, and you, too, Larry."

"Thanks, Ms. Carlson," Larry said.

"You started out making accessories for school and you turned it into a real business with a real client," Macy went on. "That's very impressive!"

"Thanks, Mom!" Chloe said. "We wouldn't have been able to do it without your help."

Macy smiled. "Well, you helped me, too—all of you. I never realized how intense my job was. But you guys have made me understand that the fashion business can be fun. Like right now! We're producing and marketing a product, and we're having a blast."

Her mother was right, Chloe thought. The radio was jamming, Manuelo was making delicious snacks, and the six of them—Chloe, Riley, Larry, Tara, Sierra, and Mom—were happily assembling Pic-Laces. At this rate, they'd have the entire order finished by dinnertime!

The phone rang. Chloe set down her half-completed Pic-Lace and prepared to race her mother to get it. But Macy made no move to rise.

Chloe grinned. Her mother was cured! Well, sort of.

Then Chloe realized what time it was. Four o'clock! "That's the radio station calling!" She knocked down her chair as she jumped to her feet and ran to the kitchen.

"Good luck, Chloe!" Tara called out.

"We're rooting for you!" Riley shouted.

Chloe grabbed the phone. "Hello?" she gasped.

"Hello, is this Chloe-from-Malibu?" the familiar voice rang out.

"Yes!" Chloe replied breathlessly.

"It's Maxine from WMBU. We've picked your final question. Are you ready to answer it to win those Crash tickets?"

No, I am *not* ready! Chloe thought, panicking.

She took a deep breath. Of course you're ready, Carlson! You spent hours on the Internet researching music trivia. You're wearing your lucky pink socks. Bring it on!

"Yes, I'm ready!" she told Maxine.

"All right, then. This is a blast from the past question, Chloe. What hit single skyrocketed the famous folk-rock group The Byrds to superstardom?" Maxine asked.

Chloe froze. The Byrds? Weren't they a group from the 1960s or something? Like in her great-great-grandparents' generation? This was a completely unfair question!

"Chloe?" Maxine prompted her gently. "You have fifteen seconds."

Tick, tick, tick. Chloe tried to think of the answer, but she had never even *heard* a Byrds song in her life. What kind of songs would a group called the Byrds record, anyway? "Fly Away with Me"? "Don't Mess with My Bird Feeder"?

Then Chloe realized that her mother had come into the kitchen and was scribbling something on the back of the latest issue of *Vogue*.

Chloe tilted her head, trying to read the smudgy brown words. "Mr Tambourine Man."

"'Mr Tambourine Man,'" Chloe said out loud.

Bells and whistles sounded over the phone—and over the radio, too. A Crash song called "It's Your Day, Baby" blasted over the airwaves.

"Chloe-from-Malibu, you're a winner!" Maxine screeched. "You and four lucky people will be going to the Crash concert this Saturday night!"

Everyone in the Carlson house began screaming, Chloe the loudest of all. She grabbed her mom and spun her around, dancing to the throbbing beat of the Crash song.

Riley, Sierra, Tara, Larry, and even Manuelo joined in. The place was rocking!

"Now all you have to decide is who to take and what to wear," Maxine said. "Congratulations, Chloe!"

As Chloe hung up, she turned to her family and friends. "I know the answer to both questions," she announced excitedly.

Riley grinned. "Well?"

"Who am I bringing to the concert?" Chloe said. "Riley, Larry, Lennon—and Mom, if you can take the time off from work," she added, gazing hopefully at her mother.

Macy smiled. "Are you kidding? I wouldn't miss going to the Crash concert with my girls for anything in the world!"

Chloe smiled. "Cool!"

"Group hug time!" Larry cried out, reaching for Riley.

"No thanks." Riley laughed and punched his shoulder playfully.

"And as for what to wear," Chloe added, "I choose my favorite pair of jeans and an Inseparables combo!"

Everyone cheered.

mary-kate olsen **ashley** olsen

so little time

Chloe
and Riley's

SCRAPBOOK

Here's a sneak peek at

so little time

Book 13
love is in the air

"Three days until V-Day!" fourteen-year-old Chloe Carlson said. "Valentine's Day!"

"You mean, three days until D-Day," her twin sister, Riley, said. "Doomsday."

Chloe and Riley were sitting in the hall at school with their friends Sierra Pomeroy and Tara Jordan on Tuesday morning.

"How can you say that, Riley?" Sierra undid her ponytail and started fluffing her wavy red hair to make it look bigger. "Don't you have a date with that guy Andrew after school today?"

"Yes," Riley admitted.

"So maybe it will be great!" Sierra said. "Maybe you'll go crazy over him! Maybe he'll be your Valentine!"

"Maybe," Riley said. "But I'm not getting my hopes up too high."

"Why not?" Tara asked.

"Yeah," Chloe said. "Andrew is totally cute. How bad could it be?"

"Oh, it could be bad," Riley said. "Reality check? Do I really have to remind you that even the cutest guys can have zero personality? Remember Cory? Last week?"

"Oh, right," Chloe said, remembering. "You didn't have such a great time with him."

"To put it mildly," Riley said. Cory was a sophomore who had asked Riley to spend an afternoon on the beach with him. "I *thought* it was a date, but maybe it wasn't," she explained to Sierra and Tara. "He seemed nice and everything. But then, while we were walking on the beach, we ran into his friends. He invited them all to come hang out with us!"

"Ouch," Sierra said.

"From then on our date was pretty much Cory and his friends playing touch football while I sat alone and watched," Riley went on. "They wouldn't even let me play!"

"That *was* pretty bad," Chloe admitted. "Oh! And there was that guy who never stopped calling you. Remember? He'd call the day before the date and say, 'Don't forget about our date tomorrow!' Then he'd call the morning of the date, half an hour before he picked you up, right after he dropped you off, an hour later, the next morning . . ."

"So you can see why I'm not that excited about my date tonight," Riley said, "or Valentine's Day."

"Well, I say give Andrew a chance anyway. You never know when the right guy will come along." Chloe said, thinking about her boyfriend Lennon Porter. "As for me? I can't *wait* for Valentine's day!"

"How are you and Lennon going to celebrate?" Tara asked.

"I don't know yet," Chloe said. "We haven't talked about it." Her blue eyes sparkled with excitement. "Do you think he'll give me a present?"

"Probably," Sierra said. "Isn't that what boys do on Valentine's Day?"

"I wonder what he'll give you," Tara said. "I wonder if anything exciting will happen!"

"Me, too," Chloe said. "Will he give me a big heart-shaped box of chocolates? Or flowers? Or a beautiful card? It's going to be so romantic!"

"We'll see," Riley warned. "Boys can be totally clueless about that stuff sometimes."

"I have a feeling Lennon will come through." Chloe grinned wide. "You guys, do you realize that this Friday is going to be my first real romantic-y boyfriend-y Valentine's Day! I am so psyched!"

The bell rang. "Homeroom. See you at lunch," Riley said as the girls split up.

Chloe picked up her books and started down the hall toward her homeroom. She spotted Lennon up ahead by his locker, talking to his friends Zach Block and Sebastian Lee.

I'll just say a quick hello, she thought as she moved closer. But she couldn't help overhearing what the boys were saying.

"So, it's this Friday. Three days away," Lennon was saying. "It's going to be so cool! But it's top secret, okay? And I totally want to surprise Chloe."

Sebastian and Zach nodded. "No problem," Zach said.

Then Sebastian looked up and saw Chloe. "Hi, Chloe," he said.

Lennon turned to face her, and Chloe couldn't help melting at the sight of him. He was so cute! Tall and lanky with intelligent blue eyes and shaggy brown hair just *this close* to needing a haircut.

"Hey," he said, smiling at her. Then he sort of glanced at the others as if to say "Don't tell!"

The second bell rang. Lennon gave Chloe a kiss on the cheek and slammed his locker door shut. "We'd better get to class," he said. "See you later!"

Chloe hugged her books to her chest as she hurried down the hall. She was so excited she thought she'd explode!

Lennon was planning a surprise for her—for Valentine's Day! It was so sweet! But Chloe could hardly stand the suspense. What could it be?

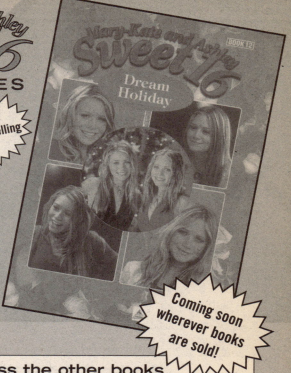

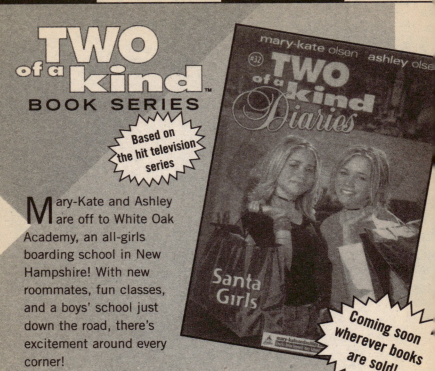

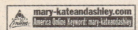

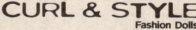